Messiah

Messiah

Martyn James Pummell

Library of Congress Control Number: 2016919447
ISBN: Hardcover   978-1-5245-9510-4
                Softcover   978-1-5245-9509-8
                eBook   978-1-5245-9508-1

Print information available on the last page.

Rev. date: 01/17/2017

To order additional copies of this book, contact:
Xlibris
800-056-3182
www.Xlibrispublishing.co.uk
Orders@Xlibrispublishing.co.uk
739144

Contents

Chapter 1

The old string and glue Dakota dropped alarmingly out of a hot Indian sky and with a lurch that almost broke its back, flopped down exhausted on the stretch of ruts and potholes that passed for a runway.

Clearing its considerable throat, it wheeled at the far end and as if running short of breath trundled a few yards and cut out.

After a suitable pause the door opened and a set of steps extruded like a poking tongue then sagged to the burnt earth as the face of a man dressed in crumpled white linen appeared in the space above.

Arthur Greene mopped perspiration from his face and picked up his suitcase. Christ, it was like stepping into an oven! In no great hurry he trundled in the direction of a cluster of huts the pilot had called the 'Terminal Buildings'. If terminal meant end the description had been accurate.

Halfway he stopped to mop his brow again, sweat was swamping his armpits and settling around his waist, a soggy money belt, and his feet were sliding in his shoes like paddling plimsolls.

He visualised that prick Bill Chalmers, squatting behind his desk with his feet up and a smirk on his asinine face, handing out advice to Marg the girl who did everything - and that meant everything. "Marg, get your tits out of that typewriter and listen to the oracle. Do you realise while we sit here contemplating whether we should duck in the toilet together and have a quick workout before lunch, our goofy friend Greene is touching down in some God-forgotten spot where syphilis grows on trees and the food is even worse? I Hope he finds his Messiah before he melts!'

Arthur seemed to have been walking forever, and the huts were disappearing in the steam bath that passed for air, and reappearing further off.

All part of the Chelmer's plan, "Park at the far end of the runway, old boy, make the bastard walk - sharpen his appetite, what?'

He glanced over his shoulder half expecting the pilot to be hanging from his window laughing. Nothing moved, only a crane stood there on spindly legs hoping there was some dick with a big bag of nuts aboard who had a weakness for oversized chickens.

The 'Terminal Buildings' were a bloody disaster built in the last century as a Turkish bath. One solitary man in a dirty dhoti, with the expression of a mortuary attendant with a deformed foot sat beside a bench still bearing the remnants of breakfast and a stain at one end that looked alarmingly like shit.

Arthur lugged his case over and parked it on the clean end.

'Greetings, brother,' he muttered.

The Customs official made no comment, but deftly flipped the lock and threw back the lid of his case, He spent ten minutes minutely examining the contents. Just as deftly he closed it and held his hand out.

Nonplussed, Arthur dug in his pocket and pulled out a small handful of change. He sorted out a ten bob note and put it in the waiting brown palm.

The Customs officer made a brief study of it before committing it to some invisible pocket. He shook his head several times. 'No, Sir, you misinterpret me entirely, I wish to see your passport.'

Arthur swore. Ten bob down the drain. He handed the required document over and watched the long sensitive fingers flip over each page from start to finish. When it was done, the officer treated him to an unhurried examination, comparing him with the photograph in the passport several times and with a sigh as if bowing to the inevitable he stamped the passport he handed it back and gave a slight bow. 'Welcome to India Sir. Do not drink the water.' He disappeared through bead curtains into the interior dragging his misshapen foot after him.

Arthur swiped a couple of flies that were enthusiastically feeding on the corners of his mouth and went out into the white heat of a baked clay road. a solitary car, a vintage Mercedes, attended by an equally vintage driver standing beside it, he plodded over and dropped the bag alongside the man who by now was bending over the engine, engrossed with the innards of the vehicle. He waited. The man could have been frozen solid. He cleared his throat and swatted at the flies again. 'I need to get to Ranpore. You take me? you know the Imperial

Hotel? Imperial Hotel,' he said pronouncing the words like an idiot child and felt like one.

The man unwound himself from the car's intestines and deliberately closed the bonnet. He turned to Arthur revealing a face like a wash leather. He touched his turban in salute. Sir Greene? Jahmel is sending me to bring you same Imperial Hotel.' He indicated himself. I am your driver. I am Achmed

Arthur slung his bag onto the back seat, and opened the front door, Achmed ran around to the passenger side, 'Please Sir Green it is important you sit in back he said with a bow, like important person I have honour among family, if big man ride in car, big man ride in back, like important person, you important man from Reuter.' As Arthur Green climbed into the back the money belt broke. 'Not Reuter, Achmed, World News.'

"Yes Sir, Reuter World News".

The old Mercedes rolled slowly across the runway and bumped its way to a lane at the back of the airfield

The country rolled by, fields, huts, wells, trees, like revolving scenery in a silent film.

"Achmed, how long Imperial?"

'Yes Sir Green, Reuter, sometime tomorrow for sure.'

Christ! thought Arthur, 24 hours in a vintage Merc, even for the new Messiah, I hope it's worth it

As the car bumped slowly along the dusty roads, Arthur reflected on the telephone call from Bill Steel that had started it all. Still in deep sleep he had cupped the phone between his ear and the pillow and reached over to switch on the bedside light. Over went the water jug, and watching the contents drip soggily onto the carpet Bill said, the old man's on his way in and he wants to see you someone called Jahmel sent in a story about some kid in the foothills of nowhere who's been bringing back the dead and feeding the five thousand, the whole Jesus bit, the old man wants you out there before some bastard crucifies him.

Arthur threw back the covers and stood up in the pool of spilt water, O K 'I'm on my way he said; he looked at the travelling clock, the one Anne had given him, she said he needed a travelling clock more than he needed her, he told her he thought she was right as she left, the clock was still going, and so was Anne, it said ten-to-three.

He got to Fleet Street in less than an hour, grabbed a bacon sandwich at Mick's and walked into the office eating it, the old man's Rolls had been outside, double parked, as usual, people were coming and going, just a normal 5am on Tuesday, he got in the lift and pressed No7.

Bill Steel was standing in the corner by the ticker-tape machine and the old man was at his desk half asleep, he got up when he saw Arthur and held out his hand and smiled like he was actually pleased to see him; 'Arthur good of you to come so soon, sit down', he picked up the phone and asked for some coffee. 'Look at this Arthur,' he held out a typed transcript, 'it came in about three hours ago,' he took the sheet and read it:

> "WORLD NEWS, FLEET STREET LONDON ENGLAND
>
> "BOY AT JAIPUR CAUSING MUCH COMMOTION AMONG PEOPLE STOP TALK OF NEW GOD STOP HAVE BEEN TO AREA TO CHECK STOP HAVE MET DISCIPLE WHO CLAIMS WAS BROUGHT BACK FROM THE DEAD STOP REPEAT DEAD STOP THEY ARE CALLING CALL HIM MESSIAH STOP.
>
> JAHMEL."

'What do you think Arthur?'

Arthur looked up, 'I don't know. If it is true it's about time, the old one has been gone for over 1900 years It's about time we had new one, I don't know what to say, but you know Bill cynic is my middle name

'Well, cynic or not, you're going out there to find out if it is true. I've laid on a plane at Croydon, Albert will take you, he's waiting downstairs, and for Christ's sake keep this one close to your chest, if there is any truth to it The Times and the Telegraph people will be onto it soon enough.

Arthur walked out of the office as a porter came in carrying a tray of coffee, and went down stairs and got in the back of the Rolls.

"You'd better drop me home first Albert I'll need a few things.' As they pulled away into the London traffic he thought back to the office, "there may be another son of God on earth, people were still talking about the first one, if he ever existed, and the old man said 'Keep quiet about it, for Christ's sake.'"

Chapter 2

Achmed brought the car to a stop and pointed out of the window, 'Rampore, Sahib Green.'

Arthur got out of the car and walked to the side of the dirt track Achmed had called a road, and looked out over the valley to a town at the foot of a tumbling range of hills, it looked dusty and dry, and melted into the country side like a desert creature, smoke spiralled into the cloudless blue sky and hung about the town like a white chiffon stoll.

Achmed walked over to Arthur, 'my home, Sir Green', Arthur smiled, 'it looks dusty,' 'yes sir, everybody's home is dusty, but you know sir home is home.

Arthur mopped his brow 'How long have you known Jahmal?' 'Since he was a boy Sir, everybody knows when a boy child is born, there is much celebration. He go to Delhi when small boy to uncle at big school, and then to England for more learning then he come back very rich and clever.'

'Do you work for him?' yes, Baba Ji 'sometime, everybody in Ranpore work for Jahmel.' 'What's he like, Arthur said as he tried to find some shade at the side of the road?' Achmed looked up into the sky and pointed, Arthur looked up as he pointed at a great Hawk floating and drifting on the spirals. Achmed touched his arm; 'don't worry, Sahib, only sick or silly rabbits get eaten,' he laughed slowly at first inside, then the laughter was too much for his body and it forced its way up to his mouth and poured out like sunlight Arthur shielded his eyes and looked up at the Hawk again and laughed. They were still laughing as they got back into the car, Achmed released the handbrake and the car rolled slowly down the dusty road.

The journey from the landing strip had taken 16 hours, it could have been done in 12 but Achmed had paraded Arthur at every village like a prodigal son, everywhere they stopped Achmed's friends and family seemed to appear out of nowhere and insist on touching Arthur, and showing him their new born babies and goats, everyone seemed to be a relation of Achmeds', they had welcomed him warmly; they had drunk tea and eaten chapatti's at what seemed like a dozen villages, at every stop they were overrun by children Achmed had called him Sir and touched him, held his arm, slapped him on the back, and laughed all the time, but when they were alone again he called him Baba Ji

The streets of Ranpore were packed with jostling crowds all trying to peer into the car, pointing at Arthur and calling to Achmed, he seemed to know them all, and talked to them through the open window, laughing and pointing at Arthur with his thumb. As the car edged through the crowd they started banging the roof of the car and chanting, 'what are they singing Achmed?' 'Oh their song says that you are very rich man from England come to buy land for Hotel, you will build big Hotel and many people come here. Make Ranpore famous, and bring wealth to the area. Ranpore is very poor town, the crops don't always come, sometimes there is not enough to eat, a big Hotel would be good for everyone. Jahmel told them you come to build Hotel.' 'Do you know why I have come Achmed ?' 'no Baba Ji, but I know it's not build Hotel.

The car stopped in front of a three storied Victorian building that looked out of place among the low flat roofed houses and bazaars. Ahmed turned around and said proudly 'Imperial Sahib, when we get out of car, I take bag, you keep hand on money, many good thieves in Ranpore.' They got out of the car, and the crowd parted to let them walk up the steps, Arthur looked up, the stucco was peeling off in places, and cracks, injuries from long past earth tremors were plastered over with mud and straw. The crowd was silent now, but still smiling; half way up in the middle of the steps an old man stood to attention, as they climbed the steps Achmed put his hand on Arthur,s arm, 'this is Ravi Sir Green,' they stopped in front of the old man, whose face exploded into a toothless grin, he was wearing a faded British army jacket, with a row of dusty medals on his chest. He stood at attention eyes front. Arthur looked at the medals, nodded at him and smiled. The old man spoke to Arthur, slowly at first as if he were remembering a speech, occasionally looking to the crowd for encouragement. 'What does he say Achmed?' 'He says he is old (Gurkha) soldier, he served the King and fought for England, he wishes to serve you now.' 'Will you thank him and tell him that he shall not serve me, but that he shall be my friend, and that we shall serve each other as friends.' As

Achmed translated Arthur felt in his pocket for some coins, and while examining the medals again dropped the coins into the tunic pocket and winked at the old man; his face split into a great smile revealing empty gums. Arthur took his bag from Achmed, walked to the top of the steps and went into the dark entrance of the Imperial. He stood in the entrance for a moment while his eyes became accustomed to the darkness, on his right next to a curly topped hat-stand was an open writing desk with a silver card tray on it, he put his bag down by the hat-stand, on the tray was a solitary card, it said Jahmel Welcomes you to The Imperial Hotel, Ranpore. Above the desk was a faded photograph of two hunters, one was kneeling down holding the head of an enormous Tiger towards the camera, the other was standing over the beast with one foot on its belly looking very pleased, beside him was a grubby Indian lad one hand on his hip, the other holding a rifle in mock hunter style, the gun was at least a foot taller than the boy. Down the centre of the hall was a faded red carpet which was disintegrating in places, it ran to the foot, of a grand sweeping stairway. The old panelled walls were thick with ancient swords and muskets, photographs of hunters and trophies, the doors leading off the hallway were of heavy oak, between each doorway was an oil lamp on a wall bracket, the heavy red velvet curtains matched the carpet and were drawn, across high windows at the end of the hall shutting out the bright evening sunlight.

Arthur turned suddenly as a door clicked at the far end of the hall, out of the darkness came a tall Indian of about fifty, he was wearing an immaculate blazer, white shirt and trousers, the colours of his tie matched the badge on his blazer pocket, he held out his hand, "Mr. Green what a pleasure it is to see someone from the old country," his teeth gleamed in the darkness. "I'm Jahmel."

"Thank you," said Arthur, "It's good to be here at last, it's been quite a journey."

"Yes, I'm afraid it is rather tiresome, but you are here now, we will have a drink while your case is unpacked." He spoke perfect English.

Jahmel opened one of the heavy oak doors and gestured Arthur to follow, they went into a small bar room. The bar ran along the wall to the left, it was richly carved with Elephants and Tigers, and had a copper inlaid top, behind the bar was a mirror edged with gold, facing the bar was a wall of drawn red velvet curtains, the wall above the bar was covered with more faded photographs of hunters and their trophy's

An old Indian man in a white serving jacket was lighting oil lamps as they came in, he turned to greet them, "Good evening, gentlemen, he said with a slight bow welcome to the Imperial how can I serve you?" His English was faultless. Jahmel guided Arthur to the bar, "May I suggest a Pimms, old chap, just the job for this wretched climate regrettably not as cold as it could be, but we have trouble with ice you know.." They sat at the bar while the old man poured the drinks. Jahmel nodded toward the old barman, "this is Charley, an absolute treasure you know, don't know what we would do without him."

Arthur looked at his reflection in the mirror, his tie was undone and pulled loose, patches of sweat showed beneath the armpits of his jacket, and his face was lined with dust, he picked up his drink and looked at Jahmel, the badge on his blazer pocket was of crossed cricket bats, ruby encrusted gold cuff links glittered on his immaculate white cuffs, and his shoes were of highly polished black and white leather. Arthur looked back into the mirror. "I'm sorry, but I didn't realise I was in such a mess. I'd better have a bath and clean myself up a bit."

"But of course, old chap, what a host! but I was so keen to hear the latest news from the old country, very selfish of me but we will have plenty of time to talk later."

Jahmel rang a small hand bell on the end of the bar, a moment later a tall thin houseboy came in and Jahmel spoke to him quickly in Indian, then turned to Arthur, "This is Gomal, he will show you to your room, your bath is already drawn, if there is anything else you need, just ring the bell in your room, Gomal will hear. "please take your drink with you, and take your time.

As Arthur was leaving the bar Jahmal called to him, "By the way, Arthur, I hope you don't think it impertinent of me, but I could not help noticing you had only an overnight bag with you, if you let Gomal have your suit, we'll have it laundered for the morning. I'll lend you something to wear for dinner, we dine at seven, you will hear the gong."

Arthur mumbled his thanks and followed Gomal up the stairway to his room.

The bedroom was large, but crowded by an enormous canopied four poster and an ornate carved mahogany wardrobe. Gomal turned up the oil lamp on a bedside table, walked across the room and went through a door opposite the bed, a few seconds later a light spilled through the doorway into the bedroom. Gomal came back and signalled to Arthur that he wanted his suit, he took off the suit and handed it to Gomal, who bowed and left the room with the suit over his arm.

Arthur took off his shoes and lit a cigarette, inhaled deeply and went through the lighted doorway. The floor struck cool to his feet, it was black marble, everything in the bathroom was black marble. The bath in the centre of the room was sunk below the level of the floor with ornate serpent head taps, and reflected the ornate oil lamps the wall opposite was completely covered by a mirror, below it was a low seat in the shape of an elephant carved from black marble. Arthur finished undressing and walked down the steps into the cool water.

As he lay in the cool bath he thought to himself with a smile 3 days from London and in another world a world of Tigers, oil lamps, dust, and faded splendour.

Was it a world that would welcome a new Messiah ?

After he finished drying himself and went back into the bedroom. Laid out neatly on the bed was a Major's uniform, shirt, tie and socks, by the bed was a pair of polished riding boots.

As Arthur straightened the khaki tie, the sound of the dinner gong drifted through the room. He looked at himself in the wardrobe mirror and decided that the cross belts and pistol was a little too militaristic for dinner. He took the gun from the leather holster, it was a Browning butt-loading .45, released the clip and it sprang into the palm of his hand. It was loaded, he replaced the magazine, slipped on the safety catch, hung it in the wardrobe and whispered to himself as he walked down the long hall, "who knows what the future holds." and went down to dinner.

Jahmel stood at the bottom of the stairs waiting for him. "Arthur, my dear fellow, you look magnificent. I hope you don't mind, but it was all we had that would fit you."

"I don't mind. Anything is better than that suit of mine, it was beginning to lead a life of its own."

Jahmel threw back his head and laughed, "good, good, that's the ticket. Come on we'll have a quick one before dinner," he put his arm around Arthurs' shoulder and still laughing they went through into the bar.

All the oil lamps were alight now and room was bright. They turned to walk to the bar, and Arthur stopped, standing in front of the bar was an Indian girl of about twenty, she was about five foot two and wore a dark blue and white Sari. Her hair fell about her shoulders black as a Ravens wing, and deep brown eyes smiled at him from a face that had been kissed golden by centuries of warm sun.

Jahmel put his arm around her. "Arthur, may I present my sister, Rhane."

Arthur held out his hand, she placed her hand in his as if she was giving him something precious, it was small and cool and as delicate as a fledgling.

"Mr. Green, we have both been looking forward to your visit for so long. I can hardly believe you are here at last. You must tell me exactly what the ladies in London are wearing just now." As she spoke, she smiled and her hair danced changing the ebony into the colour of polished copper in the soft reflection of the oil lamps her reflection echoed into the distance in the mirror behind the bar.

Arthur cleared his throat, and wondered how she could have been looking forward to his visit for so long?

"I'm afraid woman's fashions are not really my line of country, but I know large picture hats were all the rage at Ascot this year."

She laughed again and took his arm, "really, Mr. Green shame on you. Large picture hats are always the rage at Ascot, I'm sure you can do better than that if you try." They walked to the bar and she took his arm

"What will it be Arthur? gin and tonic?". Said Jahmel.

Arthur looked at Rhane, as she sat down and something in her smile reminded him of another time and another girl and the thrill of first love, and the sadness of first love lost. Of holding hands, and kisses in the dark, and promises made that were made to be broken, she reminded him all the loves of his life, from the girl he had held hands with after school, to the way his wife looked at him after he made love to her, in the early days when they had been happy.

"Gin and tonic?" he looked up, "thank you, a gin and tonic will be fine."

Gomal walked carefully from behind the bar and set the drink before him.

"Now then Rhane I'm sure Arthur does not want to talk about women's hats. What about the Test Matches? I see the Aussies kept the ashes. The Times said that Donald's field placings were to blame, but I find that hard to believe."

Arthur felt the collar of his uniform tighten. "I'm afraid I don't know much about cricket either. Jahmel looked at Arthur in silence and Rhane smiled and said, "I'm sure you are very sensible Mr Green, such a silly game."

The door opened and a houseboy came in and spoke to Jahmel. Rhane looked up and smiled at Arthur, "Dinner is ready Mr. Green, May I," she took his arm and they left the bar together.

The dining room was low, about the same size as the bar, and oak panelled, there were photographs of cricket elevens and hunters on one wall, the others were empty, but for a row of oil lamps. The table was large and round and set in the centre of the room; next to the table were two ice buckets on stands. Arthur held Rhane's chair as she sat down, and then sat in the opposite chair. Jahmel was busy sorting through a wine rack which stood next to an oak Welsh dresser at the far end of the room.

"I hope this evening will prove to you that we are able to enjoy the finer things in life, Jahmel said as he sat down. "We will start with an insignificant fresh water fish, however, it will be complimented by a Chablis of Noble birth, a '29' that would make even a Sari taste like an oyster," he smiled at his joke. "Followed by a fillet of beef that I'm sure will surprise you, closely supported by a Le Chambertin '32', cheese, fresh fruit, coffee, cognac and cigars."

"It sounds a meal fit for a king," said Arthur. "I think my stomach would mutiny at one more chapatti."

Jahmel looked pleased, you will have seen Mr Green the we adopt a European diet here, more in the British tradition.

The door opened and three houseboys carrying trays came in and served the first course, while Jahmel took a bottle from the ice bucket, opened it, and poured it.

"I'm afraid we have no ice, but the wine has been resting in a stream that comes from the mountains for a few hours, I'm sure you will find it sufficiently chilled."

Arthur took a sip, started to eat
. "Do you know England well, Rhani?"

"Yes, very well, although I have never been there, she smiled Jahmel has told me everything about it, and we take the English newspapers, when we can get them, I feel that I'm quite an authority, I could describe the 'Cafe Royal' better than the Manager. Do you know it?"

"I have been there."

"Is the cocktail bar still through to the left after the entrance?"

"I believe so said Arthur, but it is a long time since I was there."

"And are there still two steps down to the restaurant? and is everything covered in red velvet?" She looked past Arthur as she spoke, and seemed far away. "I can see it now, all the fine gentlemen in dinner suits, and the ladies, their long dresses brushing the floor, the waiters bowing, the candle light dancing on the glasses."

Jahmel rapped his glass with a spoon. "Drink your wine, Arthur knows the damn place well enough I'm sure."

"I don't know it well," said Arthur, "certainly not as well as Rhani." Arthur said with a smile turned to Jahmel, "I understand you went to school in England?"

"Yes, I had that honour. I was at Cambridge for five years, The best five years of my life."

"It's a long way from Rhanpore to Cambridge," said Arthur, trying to draw Jahmel.

"Yes," said Jahmel, as he topped up the glasses, "but I don't want to bore you."

"Please," said Arthur. "It may be background for an article sometime.

Jahmel sat quietly sipping his wine for a few moments, then left the table and went out into the hall. He returned carrying a framed photograph and held it in front of Arthur. It was the one from above the desk that he had noticed as he entered the Hotel, of the two hunters and the small boy. Jahmel left it on the table and sat down.

"When that photograph was taken this Hotel was in its heyday. It was always full of gentlemen, English gentlemen, and sometimes their ladies."

The houseboys were clearing away the remains of the first course as he spoke.

"I have known many countries in my life. I travelled extensively throughout Europe after Cambridge, you know. I think German aggression caused wars that we are still recovering from, they tried to assert themselves and rule Europe through their industrial power. And the French, since Napoleon's time have become hedonistic and weak more interested in their vineyards and pleasure. The English, the English are strong, leaders, really strong, through assurance and self-belief. and their own industrial strength

He leaned over to Arthur, "they stand like Judo experts in the pub of Europe, they have no fear."

A houseboy came in carrying a steaming slab of beef as Jahmel left the table and went to the bar and picked up an ornate crystal decanter with a silver collar and brought it to the table it and filled a glass in front of Arthur. "The only good thing to come out of France is wine, and this is the King, Chambertan." He filled the other glasses, returned to his seat and started to carve the beef.

"You see the boy?" he nodded at the photograph on the table. "That's me, the gentleman holding the Tiger's Head is Sir William Hollingsworth, the one standing is Colonel Sir Cyril Coleman. They came for the tigers, you know."

"How old were you?" Arthur said as he took a plate piled high with beef.

"I was seven. About three months before that photograph was taken my family, who were poor people, received a letter from an uncle in Delhi offering to take over my education, which up to that time had been non-existent. He was a trader, in silks and spices and very wealthy, for him it was a gesture; for my family it meant one less mouth to feed. What do you think of the wine, Arthur?"

"It's excellent, a lovely temperature, what happened then?"

"I arrived in Delhi hardly able to speak Indian, let alone English. I went to the Colonial Day College, and it was there surrounded by the sons of English gentlemen that I met a remarkable man, Professor James. He also gave me private tuition at my Uncles' home at the same time, he had been a Tutor at Cambridge, and he used to tell me tales of the University as we studied, of the colleges, the brilliant men they had produced, the Rugby matches and the boat race against Oxford, punting on the Cam, the tea shops in the town, cricket matches, the splendid rags, I knew every weathered stones years before I went."

Gomal circled the table filling the glasses. "I remember one weekend in London in particular, my good friend was Pinky Wilson. He had red hair and white skin that went pink if he was in the sun too long, Admiral Wilson's son you know, he had made the University Eight, and was to row against Oxford that year, and his father bought him a Bentley to celebrate, 4½ litres Villiers supercharged, went like a bomb. Well we decided to spend the weekend in London to celebrate, and" he looked at Rhani, "I think I had better finish that story later. Well, anyway, I finished my studies at Cambridge, left with a first class Honours degree and travelled Europe for a while; about two years later my Uncle died and left me his estate. I returned home and bought the Imperial.

At first I only employed English speaking houseboys, but the Tigers were harder and harder to find and the gentlemen stopped coming and one by one they left, there is only Gomal left now."

The houseboys started to clear away the remains of the dinner, and brought a basket filled high with fruit and set it in the centre of the table. Another wheeled in an ornate trolley set with various cheeses.

Arthur pushed his chair back
, "I'm finished, I could not eat another mouthful, it has really been a most memorable meal."

"Coffee then," said Jahmel, and spoke to the houseboys, who immediately cleared the table. He had not spoken to Rhani all evening, and did not consult her now.

"Have you seen the boy?" they call the Messiah? asked Arthur turning to Rhani trying to draw her into the conversation.

Jahmel answered. "Yes, she has seen the boy, we'll talk of that later."

Rhani did not answer. but looked down at the table careful not to catch Arthur's eye.

A houseboy set the coffee tray before Rhani, and a humidor before Jahmel. He opened the box, selected a cigar, cut the end with a gold cigar cutter and handed it to Arthur. A houseboy held a heavily chased silver candelabra for Arthur as he lit his cigar, then set it in the centre of the table.

Jahmel spoke to Rhani in Indian, and glanced at Arthur, she looked at him. "I am sure you will excuse me," she said, "but I am feeling a little tired."

Arthur stood up as she moved, she went to her brother and kissed his cheek. As she left the room she said to Arthur. "I'll see you in the morning." She spoke deliberately, putting more meaning into the words than the casual sentence implied.

Jahmel was at the bar and selected another decanter. now then I have an excellent cognac that will crown the meal."

"Not for me," Arthur protested. "I'm afraid I am feeling the effects of the wine."

"Nonsense, nonsense, it's a fine Napoleon Brandy and will settle your stomach."

He poured the Brandy and returned to the table and sat in Rhani's chair, and held his glass over the candle flame, warming it.

Arthur looked into his glass, it was rich and golden, the candle light danced on it. "What about the boy, Jahmel? I don't want to spoil the evening, but I am working, and I have to produce a story or go home."

"Produce a story, produce a story!" Jahmel repeated his words. He leaned across the table. "Arthur, you'll produce a story alright, a story that will make you famous. A story that will make Rhanpore famous. A story that will fill the Imperial. A story," he said the words half to himself. "God's son is asleep not six miles from here, and you talk about a story." Jahmel drained his glass, and refilled it. "Drink up, old chap," he topped up Arthur's glass. Do you play billiards?"

"Yes, but I prefer snooker."

Jahmel laughed, "the cad's game. Very well we will play snooker."

"I think I had better get some sleep," said Arthur. "It's been a long day, and I want to be reasonably fresh tomorrow."

"Fresh," said Jahmel, "Fresh, ah yes, fresh for the boy, the Messiah." He was drunk now, he stood up and put one hand on the table, "we will play snooker and I will tell you about the young Raj, The Messiah. You know nothing of him and I know everything."

Arthur sipped the cognac, his head was aching, he was starting to feel the effects of the wine

"Very well, but first may I have some more coffee?"

Jahmel shouted some instructions, a few moments later a houseboy came in carrying another tray of coffee.

Jahmel put their glasses and the decanter on the tray and went to a door that was concealed in the oak panelling, near the dresser. Arthur followed, "you take the tray, old chap, I'll light the lamps." Arthur stood in the doorway holding the tray, and they went into the darkness. As he struck the first match to light the lamps shadows bounced about the room. Tigers heads snarled from the walls then disappeared in the flickering light. The lamps were lit till the room was full of light. There were three or four stuffed Tigers heads on each wall surrounding the table. Jahmel took the tray from Arthur and put it on a table, then went to the billiards table and pulled back the cover.

As Jahmel set up the balls, Arthur looked at the Tiger's Head nearest to him, underneath it was a brass plaque mounted on polished wood, on it was engraved; ' Colonel Sir Cyril Coleman, 1929'. Arthur laughed to himself, doesn't look anything like him.

"Heads or tails?"

"Heads" called Arthur, and selected a cue from the rack.

"You break," said Jahmel.

Arthur sent the white ball past the pack slowly, it screwed back and nestled gently into the reds.

"What about the boy?"

Jahmel selected a cue, sat on the edge of the table, his right foot just touching the floor. He played away from the pack, the ball ran off the side cushion, on to the top cushion, and came to rest behind the black.

"He lives about six miles from here on a bankrupt Tea Plantation."

Arthur played the ball off the side cushion, it hit the red pack and ran down the table and stopped between the brown and yellow.

"I think you've left me one," said Jahmel, circling the table. The red at the top right hand corner had been pushed clear. He bent over his cue, the white rifled up the table and hit the red with a crack, it disappeared into the top left hand pocket, the white ran onto the cushion slowly, rebounded and stopped in line with the black.

"He's about sixteen years old, an Indian village lad." The black rifled into the same pocket, the white bounced off the top and side cushions, and smashed into the reds, splitting the pack.

"We first started to hear the rumours a few months ago, didn't take much notice at first, this is a country of religious fanatics you know, there is always somebody climbing up ropes or eating nails, but the rumours kept growing. Had a servant here, no life in one arm, injured it when he was a child, an Ox stamped on it or something, he went up there, came back fit enough to make the first eleven. Gave in his notice and went back to be a disciple."

Jahmel crouched over his cue, the red banged into the top right hand pocket and the white stopped dead. He walked briskly around the table and potted the pink in the middle pocket, the white screwed back. He played a red to the top right hand pocket, but it clipped the cushion and ran down the side like a mouse along a skirting board.

"15," said Jahmel, and walked to the scoreboard.

Arthur played a red into the centre pocket, and then sent the blue after it. He repeated the play, red in the centre followed by the blue. "What about the local people," said Arthur, "how are they taking it?" What do they think?

Jahmel poured another brandy and drank it. "A lot of them are up there hanging about the plantation. The boy walks among them each day, healing and preaching.

He preaches against organised religion, says that self-religion will save the world, that each person should adopt a standard of behaviour towards his fellow man and follow it."

Arthur played a long red into the bottom left hand pocket and screwed back onto the black.

"He calls it the religion of mankind."

Arthur potted the black, and miss-cued his next red shot.

"Twenty," said Jahmel, and put up the score on the ornate brass and wood scoreboard

Arthur walked over to the side table and poured himself a coffee. "How long has this been going on?"

"The plantation is managed by an English couple. They're both getting on a bit and seem to have lost interest in it now. They say that about a year ago, during a particularly bad storm, I remember the storm actually, and it was one of the worst, the clouds are very low here, they roll down from the hills, and when it thunders it sounds like the sky is opening up. The storm lasted all night and the next morning a child's body was found on the edge of the plantation badly mutilated, it had been attacked by a tiger. Very odd really, there have been no reports of tigers in this area for many years.

Well, from that time the boy had changed, although he looked the same he was different, up to then he had been an ordinary peasant lad, but after the storm, he spent time talking with the village elders and it transpired he could speak several languages, only a little at first, it was thought he had been changed or damaged by the monsoon storm, he sought out the learned men in the area, and spent hours with them.

Shortly after that the first miracle occurred, I went up there to investigate a couple of weeks ago. The plantation managers a Mr & Mrs. Wilson didn't know much about him, they said he was the son of a native woman who died shortly after his birth. He was raised by a plantation mother with her own children, nobody knew the father. That's really all I know.

I've arranged for Achmed to take you there tomorrow, I'm afraid I have to go to Delhi for a few days, but Rhani will go with you."

Arthur stood his cue in the rack. "I hope you'll excuse me, Jahmel I am all in, I am seeing two snooker balls instead of one and I really must get some sleep."

As Arthur left the room, Jahmel looked annoyed. Arthur walked through the dining room and into the hall. and he thought of spending some hours alone with Rhani the next day excited him.

He went upstairs and into his bedroom. He started to undress, awkwardly, he was more than a little drunk, he thought about the evening, about Rhani, and the Imperial, a little outpost of England in the heart of India. He lay back on the bed and closed his eyes. He was slipping into the murky swamp of sleep, it was creeping up over his legs, he struggled to free himself. Something was wrong. What was wrong? What was it? The dark waters of sleep were lapping over his face, as he tried to free himself.

. The bar! Rhani!. So long, Mr. Green, we've both been looking forward to your visit for so long. So long.!

Chapter 3

Arthur woke with a start. A shaft of sunlight had found its way through the heavy curtain sending a shaft of sunlight across his bed. He sat up, he was still dressed in the uniform, the oil lamp was smoking and the smoke was hanging in the air and irritating his eyes, he walked to the window and threw back the curtains and opened the window and the sounds of the square flooded into the room, the small square in front of the hotel was starting to get busy, the traders were setting up their stalls, mostly they were piled with fruit and vegetables, but some had silks and other materials on them, and some spices In the corner of the square a small boy was sitting, he had no arms, a begging bowl was on the ground in front of him and he called at the people as they passed him, and looked with great sad eyes. In the shadows of the square people were sleeping curled up on the ground, shabby blankets pulled up over their heads.

Achmed was standing with a group of traders talking and waving his arms about. As they talked a group of Indians walked slowly up the street and into the square. There were about twenty of them, men and women of mixed ages, with half a dozen children. Two of the younger men were pulling a cart that was piled with bed rolls, blankets and pots and pans. They stopped near one of the traders and were obviously asking the way. He pointed to a road that led through the town, and they started in that direction, the children chasing each other around the stalls as they went.

There was a knock on the door and Charley came in.

"Good morning, sir. Did you sleep well?"

"Good morning, Charley, yes, very well, but I had a dream which almost woke me. I remember a noise, a whinnying noise, scuffling and sniffing and yapping, like dogs."

"Oh, that wasn't a dream, sir, that would be the wild dogs, nothing to worry about, they come into the town quite often at night, scavenging for food.

I see you had a heavy night sir," he said and nodded at the uniform and smiled.

"Yes, Jahmel was an excellent host, that's what my headache tells me anyway."

"A nice bath and some breakfast will put you right, sir."

Arthur started to undress and Charley ran the bath. "How long have you worked here, Charley?"

"About twenty years, sir. Ever since I came to India. I was born in England you know. My parents had a restaurant in the Tottenham Court Road. When my father died we sold the restaurant, and with my share of the money I came out here on holiday. Jahmel used to eat at our place when I was a boy, knew my father quite well. I bumped into him in Bombay, quite by accident, he had just bought this place and was looking for staff, so here I am. It was supposed to be for a few months till he got the staff trained, but I'm still here. I was alright at first, the Hotel was always full, mostly with his friends from London and Cambridge, but as the Tigers disappeared, so did they."

"Jahmel must be a very wealthy man to be able to run this place just for fun. Just because he likes the English way of life; the wages alone must come to a fortune."

"Wages, sir?" he laughed. "We haven't had wages for a long time."

"Why do you stay?"

"The houseboys stay because they get their food and somewhere to sleep, it's better than begging."

"What about you?"

"Well sir, I'm in charge of purchasing the provisions and the general running of the place. I make enough for my humble needs by shopping around, sir. When you work in a place for twenty years, it becomes a part of you, and you become part of it. I don't know what I would do if I left here, I'd feel like an Indian if I went back to the U K, and if I stayed I'd only work in another hotel, so I might as well stay here."

"What about Rhani? It seems strange for such a beautiful girl to stay out here in the middle of nowhere, being so quiet, I mean."

"Yes, sir, I know what you mean, but wherever Jahmel is, she is, it's as simple as that, she worships him. I have often told her she would do well in England.

Jahmel has raised her to be a real English Miss, but she'd never leave him, she looks on him more like a father than a brother. They

21

have been telling each other that the old place will be full again, just like the old days for so long now that I think they both believe it.

If you'd like to take your bath now, sir, I'll fetch your suit and then it will be time for breakfast."

Rhani was sitting in the Hall waiting for him as he came down the stairs. The front door was open and the street noises were drifting in. She jumped up when she saw him, she was wearing a white shirt, judpurs, and brown riding boots.

"Arthur, I hope I may call you Arthur. Did you sleep well? I've decided that we shall go riding this morning, it is no use going to the plantation until this afternoon. The Messiah spends the mornings in meditation and with the people, he is more likely to see you this afternoon, so this morning we will ride, and I will show you something of India."

"Alright, said Arthur but only if you promise that we shall see the boy this afternoon. I must see the boy I have come a long way to see him.

"Yes, Arthur, we realise perfectly well how important it is, but if you cannot see the boy this morning it is pointless to go isn't it?"

They walked through into the dining room, the table was set for two, side by side. Arthur sat down, she said, "We above all realise how important it is."

"The boy may mean a new beginning, another chance for all of us."

"What makes you think he is really the son of God?"

"When you see him you will know, there will be no doubt. And who but the Son of God could bring a man back from the dead?"

"Do you know the man?"

"No, but I have spoken to him and the miracle was performed in front of the plantation workers, there is no doubt." A houseboy came in and spoke to Rhani, she turned to Arthur, "What would you like for breakfast, Arthur?"

"Just some tea and a little toast will be fine, thank you." She spoke to the boy and he left the room.

"Are you married Arthur?"

"Sort of, my wife has left me. When God's are discovered in India it is my job to go and find out if it is true. She preferred someone with more stable employment."

Rhani put her hand on Arthur's arm, "You must be very lonely while you are here, I will do my best to see that you are not lonely."

The houseboy returned carrying a silver tray with a large pot of tea and a plate of toast on it, and set it before Rhani. When they had finished breakfast Rhani said, "I've told Charley to put some jodhpurs and riding boots in your room. If you would like to change, we can go for our ride. There is a Mosque I'd like to show you, a Temple built for a God, it is called the Pearl Mosque and cost a fortune to build, in it is a priceless pearl. The Basti people, the poor people, sometimes mutilate their children so that they will make more pitiful beggars, then they go to worship their God at a fabulous Temple with a priceless pearl in it. I think if a new God has come it is not too soon."

"It would make a great difference to you, Rhani, if the boy was genuine, wouldn't it? The Imperial would be like it was in the old days?"

"Not such a difference to me, I don't remember the old days, but to Jahmel it would, he misses the people who came from England."

They finished the meal in silence then Arthur went up to his room and changed.

Rhani was waiting for him at the bottom of the stairs again; she was holding two riding crops and she handed him one. As they left the Hotel she said, "The stables are on the edge of the town, it is a short walk."

Outside the square was busier now, and full of people, they pushed their way through the crowded streets and crossed the square, as they passed the beggar boy Arthur stopped in front of him and put his hand in his pocket. Rhani tapped his arm with her riding crop. "When you put your coppers in that bowl remember there may be a Father who sees you, and he may think to himself, that cripple boy does well from begging, and he may go and chop off the hand of his son."

Arthur looked down at the boy, at the great sad eyes and threw some coins into the bowl. "We must do what we can," he said. "I cannot be blamed for a father's ignorance; we can't change the way things are."

"Some of us, a few of us, the great ones can," she said.

They walked out of the square and down an ally, then turned into a narrower one where the bamboo and mud houses left scarcely enough room to walk between them. At the bottom was a large field, on the far side of the field was a great Mango tree, in the shade of the tree was a shed with a red corrugated iron roof, next to it two saddled horses were tethered, around the edge of the field was a deep ditch.

"What's that for? "Arthur said indicating the ditch.

"It is a monsoon ditch. It is to channel the water away from the houses and roads."

They walked along the edge of it until they came to some planks that crossed into the field, and followed a worn path to the giant tree. A boy ran from the hut and held the horses while they mounted, Rhani turned her horse and headed toward the open country and shouted with a laugh, Don't worry Arthur you horse is old and very safe, after they had been riding for about half an hour they came to a river, along its banks women in brightly coloured Saris were doing their washing, pounding the clothes against boulders. Rhani pointed at them, "those are called Dhobis, the launderers, "they crossed the river on the other side, a gang of men were clearing a monsoon ditch. She pointed at them with her riding crop. Those men must be very brave, we are near a jungle that the natives call the Place of the Gods, they think that it is where the Gods are born, they will want extra money for working this side of the river.

They rode on, the sun was getting hot now and Arthur was starting to ache. Rhani turned to him, "at the top of the hill you will see the Temple." They rode to the top of the hill, below them set in the middle of a wide valley was the Pearl Mosque. It was surrounded by a high wall of arches, tall towers rose from each corner, the centre was a great dome that tapered to a high spire.

"There it is," said Rhani, as she dismounted and sat on a great boulder. Arthur dismounted and sat next to her.

"It took fifty years to build, the cost of it would have fed a thousand families for those fifty years, and the starving people come here to worship."

Arthur looked down at the great Mosque. It was made of white marble and glinted in the sunlight.

"It looks as if it will last forever he said" She looked at him, her hair shone and hung about her shoulders, framing her face, she still looked clean and fresh. She took Arthur's arm and pulled him to her, her body felt firm and young.

"If you decided that the boy is the Son of God, there would be no use for it. If India could be united under one religion, the people would tear it down. The Messiah has no use for Temples." She parted her lips, put her hand behind his head and pulled his mouth on to hers. He kissed her gently, for a long time. They parted without speaking and remounted their horses. She led the way down gently the hill home towards the Imperial.

They left their horses in the shade of the great Mango tree and walked across the field towards the town. The sun was higher now. In the corner of the field a great Ox was walking an endless circle, a rope ran from its neck to a centre pole dictating the arc beneath its plodding feet there were piles of grain stalks. A boy was sitting in the shadow of a broken wall, naked but for a cloth wrapped around his middle; he got up slowly and raked over the crushed grain, a great black cloud of flies rose from the animal's head as he drew near. Arthur and Rhani walked on to the edge of the field and crossed the monsoon ditch over the planks and walked towards the shadows of the town.

Rhani spoke to some men that were sitting cross legged in the dust splitting bamboo canes, the canes were split and laid flat on the ground. A boy was passing some twine through the slats weaving in and out. They used their feet like hands, pulling and pushing the tough bamboo, their turbaned heads bobbing as they worked. The boy got up and walked over to Arthur and spoke to him shyly.

Arthur took the boy's hand and walked to where Rhani spoke to the men. "What did he say, Rhani?"

She spoke with the boy for a minute. "He says that they are his brothers and have gathered here today to repair their parents' house. They have left their work in the fields and will receive no pay today. If you would build a new Hotel here life would be easier for everyone. The visitors would spend money in the town. He says he would work at the Hotel in the kitchen."

When Rhani had finished speaking the boy returned to his brothers and started to work again.

They walked on; further up the street shades had been drawn and almost touched each other across the narrow road, beneath the shades women sat leaning against the buildings, embroidering silk. The square was almost empty, the stalls were gone; the sun was overhead now and there was no shade. The Imperial looked unreal, a cracked and peeling giant sleeping in the midday sun. Inside the Hotel the curtains had been drawn and it seemed cool and dark after the heat and brightness of the town.

Rhani put her riding crop on the desk. "Would you like a drink, Arthur, it's cool in the bar and we can talk until it's time to go. Or would you rather rest?"

"No. I'd like a drink, I'm thirsty. I've never seen such dry country."

"Yes, it is dry now, but the monsoons will come soon and then the roads will be like rivers.

They walked through into the bar, Charley was polishing glasses. "Good morning, sir. Good morning, madam. Did you have a good ride?"

"Yes thank you, Charley. I showed Mr. Green the Pearl Mosque, I think he was impressed."

"I was impressed, but what impressed me more was the permanence of everything, I've never known a feeling like it it's as if I had been here before, I felt as if I had been here for ever."

Charley placed two long drinks onto the bar. "Yes, sir that's India, some people feel it, some don't." They took their drinks and sat in a corner of the bar.

"How long will Jahmel be away?"

"Two days, perhaps three. Do you know why he has gone to Delhi?"

"No, except that he has gone for business reasons."

"Delhi is the headquarters of a society called Mughals They are very important and influential. Many Government Ministers belong to the Mughals also many rich business men. They are patriots, it is their aim to raise India from a land of poverty, to make it a great industrial nation, independent; they are behind the anti-British riots. A week ago Jahmel received a message saying they wanted to see him. He hates them because they want the British out, but when the Mughal send for you, you go."

"What about you, Rhani, how do you feel towards the British?"

"They have done their best, but India is too much for a small island in the North Sea to rule, they will go soon. I'm only concerned with India, and what will be best for my country. Jahmel raised me as an English girl, but I'm Indian at heart and always will be. I love this country with my heart, my soul and my body, it is part of me and I'm part of it."

She got up. "I will show you something."

Arthur followed her into the hall and up the stairs. She walked past Arthur's room and down the hall, turned the corner and opened a door. They went into the room, it was dark and musty, Rhani walked to the window and opened the curtains. It was a nursery, on the wall was a blackboard with half completed sums and in a child's hand I LOVE INDIA, beneath it was a rocking horse. Below the window was a child's desk, a toy chest stood in one corner, a doll's arm poking out holding the lid up. She walked to the rocking horse and pushed it, it nodded backwards and forwards dust motes rising in the sunlight. "When I was a child I sat there," she pointed at the desk. "Jahmel taught me English, I wore English dresses and had my hair in plaits. I used to look out of the window and watch the ragged children playing in the dust and wished I was one of them."

"You must have been very unhappy."

"I suppose I was, but this was all I knew." She waved her arm around the room. As Jahmel told me of Pinkie Wilson's Bentley, all the time I wanted to hold the oxen as the men loaded the cart."

She moved close to Arthur, she brushed his hand with hers. "I say I must be boring you, I will go and change now. It will soon be time to go."

Arthur took her in his arms, she clung to him like a child.

"Arthur, you know I could never leave India, don't you?"

He held her closer, I think I know that, I know."

The sound of a car horn broke the silence. Arthur left Rhani and went to the window.

Achmed was standing below next to the Mercedes. He turned to Rhani, "It's time to go." She straightened herself. "Very well, I'll go and change, and see you downstairs." She turned and left the room. Arthur closed the curtains and went downstairs.

Achmed was standing in the hall now, talking to Ravi, the old soldier. He left Ravi and came to the stairway as Arthur came down. "Hello, Baba Ji, we go to the plantation, yes?"

"Yes, Achmed, but Rhani is coming. She is dressing, she'll be down in a minute."

"Yes, Baba Ji."

Ravi spoke to Achmed and made a pushing sign with his hands' Ji, Ravi says that he should go with you, the journey takes us near the place of the God's, he says you may need him to protect you." Ravi straightened up as Achmed spoke and stood at attention.

Arthur walked to the old man and put his hand on his shoulder. "Tell him that we shall be pleased to have his protection."

The stairs creaked, Arthur turned it was Rhani. Arthur stopped when he saw her. Her body, arms and head were covered with a dark blue Sari that framed her face, he'd never seen her looking more beautiful. He wanted to hold her and tell her that everything would be all right.

She smiled at Arthur and Achmed and walked to Ravi, wiping the dust from his medals with the end of her sari. She then brushed his hair across his head like he was a naughty boy. When she had finished, she turned and smiled, "Shall we go?"

They walked to the car and got in, Arthur and Rhani in the back, Ravi sitting next to Achmed. he started the car and they edged their way across the square. It was getting busy again now, and the people parted and let the car through. They soon cleared the town and were on the open road. They drove slowly down the bumpy track past the field with the Mango tree and out into the countryside down a winding road that was lined by dusty fields. Monsoon ditches followed each side of the road, past carts pulled by tired ox, lazy drivers flicking them with long bamboo canes. There were groups of people camping on each side of the road. They waved at the car as it passed; on the road people were walking towards the plantation, their belongings strapped to their backs.

After about half-an-hour Achmed stopped and pointed, the country had started to get hilly now, and in the darkness Arthur could see the plantation, it rose in tiers up a hill, the tea bushes unruly and wild, unkempt. By the side of the road was a large wooden board, on it Arthur could just read the words, 'Plantation of the Rising Moon', in faded white paint.

Achmed drove on through the low ground and up the hill, they stopped at an open place, filled with people sitting cross legged quietly talking. On the far side about two hundred yards away was a European style bungalow raised from the ground on an iron frame. The crowd stopped talking and stared at them as the car came to a halt. Rhani and Arthur got out of the car and started to weave their way across the clearing. Achmed and Ravi stayed in the car.

They climbed the steps that led up to the bungalow and stepped on to the wide veranda that ran around the building. Rhani told Arthur to wait, and she opened the front door and went in. Arthur sat in a cushioned wicker-work chair with a high back and looked out at the people seated on the ground, they were silent now, and stared back at him. All the time more people were arriving, walking past the parked car, some of them pulling off their shoulder packs and falling exhausted to the ground in front of the bungalow. Some of those already there went to them, and gave them water from a goat skin gourds and gave them bundles of clothes to rest their heads on and blankets. There were several fires burning, the smoke rose lazily into the sky, and the acrid smell filled the air.

The front door opened and Rhani came out. Arthur rose to meet her, but Rhani went down the steps and signalled Arthur to follow. They seated themselves in the dust in front of the bungalow and Rhani said, "He is going to welcome the people, but we can talk with him later." Almost immediately the door opened. A tall dark-skinned boy came out onto the veranda, dressed in a white robe that ran from his shoulders to the ground. The whiteness of the robe contrasted his dark skin, he moved, it seemed to Arthur, glided to the edge of the veranda, there was no movement on the robe as he walked, his face was almost beautiful; long black hair fell to his shoulders, his eyes were large and brown.

From different parts of the clearing people were shouting now, some were standing and clapping; there was a general movement in the crowd behind them and the air was filled with excitement. Arthur felt it in himself, he was breathing quickly now as if he'd been running.

The boy raised his arms and the white robe spread out from his body, like wings, he looked around the crowd, and they fell silent under his gaze. Arthur stared at the boy unable to move, the boy in turn looked into the face of everyone before him, then his eyes met Arthur's just for a second. Arthur felt something, something he could not explain, a lightness almost a revelation, that rippled through his body and made him light headed and gasp almost frightened, for a moment; the eyes held his, and he recognised, could it be recognised, something from long past deep in the eyes. There seemed to be another life, a chance, an opportunity, an offered salvation in that glance. The eyes passed on, but the feeling of recognition stayed with Arthur; the boy moved down the steps and walked into the crowd, he talked softly as he went; some of the crowd touched his hands as he passed them.

Arthur nudged Rhani, "What is he saying?"

"He is welcoming them and asking where they have come from, and telling them to rest."

He walked on through the crowd to the edge of the clearing and stopped in front of a man sitting alone beneath a Mango tree. By the man a dung fire burned, the thick smoke hanging in the lower branches of the tree, he talked with the man for a minute then sat next to him in the dust.

Rhani said, "that man is an outcast, an untouchable, he is alone because the others will have nothing to do with him. He cannot worship in their Temples, if they ever touched him they would become outcasts too."

The boy took the man's water gourde from the pile of belongings and drank from it, then poured the water over the man's feet, then dried them with his robe. He stood up and helped the man to his feet, then arm in arm they walked back through the crowds towards the bungalow, the boy talking and smiling as they walked. When they were nearer, Rhani said, "He is telling them that the man is his brother, that he is the brother of all of them, that the caste system is wrong, why should they feel superior to this man, that they were born of superior caste was no reflection on the way they should treat their fellow men, their brothers. Some were born clever, some stupid, the circumstances of their birth came from no effort on their behalf, so why should they feel superior or inferior; that the only pride they should feel was from their efforts to be better men."

They stopped near the bungalow by a group seated around a fire, they moved closer together, making room for the man to sit down. He sat down, the boy turned and walked up the steps of the bungalow onto the veranda, turned to face the crowd and started to speak.

"I bring you greetings from my Father, He created the earth and put man on it in the hope that they would extend the boundaries of heaven, He gave men hearts so that they can spread love and humility, but while some men feel that they are better than others there can be no love, no humility. He gave them minds so that they can think how to make a better world, but they only think for their own advancement. He gave them bodies so that they may work and work for each other, but they work for themselves, they build Temples, not for God, but for themselves, there are no Temples in Heaven. I come to bring you the religion of man, you must forget the caste system, black must marry white, caste must marry caste in India, and the world. Only true love can save the World, without true integration the World will not survive; my Father grows tired, He will soon test the earth, only true love can save it." The boy closed his eyes for a minute in prayer, then turned and went into the bungalow.

Arthur looked at Rhani and took her hand, "I don't know if He is the Son of God, but what he says makes sense."

She smiled at him, "You will soon believe like the rest of us."

Arthur looked around, the crowd were starting to disperse now, he could see Achmed and Ravi seated on the edge of the clearing. Rhani got up and went into the bungalow, a few minutes later she came to the door and signalled Arthur to come in. As Arthur entered the bungalow a shadow fell across him, he looked up at the sky, dark clouds were passing across the dipping sun, bringing a cool breeze. He went through the door and entered an English lounge, a table laid for tea, a sideboard with willow pattern plates on it, on the wall a photograph of the King in uniform. By the table stood Mr and Mrs Wilson, she was dressed in a simple sari, he in a white shirt, the sleeves rolled up and grey trousers. Rhani held out her hand, "Arthur, this is

Mr and Mrs Wilson, Mr and Mrs Wilson, Mr. Arthur Green." Arthur shook hands with them. Mrs Wilson smiled a motherly smile and said with the hint of a north country accent, "You are welcome Mr Green, I hope you will stay for tea."

Arthur said he would be pleased to. Mr Wilson said, "Sit down over here, Mr Green," he signalled to two easy chairs by the window, "we can talk while the girls get the tea ready."

As they sat down, Mr Wilson pulled a pipe from his pocket and started to clean it.

"You know why I am here Mr Wilson?"

"Yes, you've come to write about our boy, that's a figure of speech of course, but we have always treated him as a son, we have no children of our own you know."

"How long is that?"

"Since shortly after he was born. His mother died and he was adopted by a native woman who worked for us, they lived here with us in the bungalow. A couple of years later she died, if they are working in the fields they don't live very long out here you know; the wife has looked after him since then. He says that he's only been on earth for a year or so since the storm, but we have looked after him since he was a child very strange that, but I don't pretend to understand it all."

"When did you first realise that he was special, not like other people?"

"About a year ago, there was a chap that came here with his wife. She picked the tea in the plantation and he did general maintenance work, fences and that sort of thing. One day soon after the storm he came back to the bungalow early and complained of feeling sick and went to lie down. In the evening I went to see how he was. He was dead, there was no doubt, his heart had stopped and there was no pulse, in India you soon get to recognise death. I went to his people and told them so that they could arrange the burial and the service. When I came back Mrs Wilson told me that Frank was with him. We've always called him Frank, we would have called our son Frank, if we'd had one. Shortly after that the door opened and they both came out; the man was alive and well, that was the start of it really."

Mrs Wilson and Rhani came in from the kitchen, one carrying a plate of bread and butter, the other a large pot of tea and a pot of jam.

Mrs Wilson said, "come along Fred, don't let the tea get cold, you boys can talk later."

As they sat down Mrs Wilson said, "what part of London do you come from, Mr Green?"

"From Hackney, it's in the East End.

Will Frank be joining us?"

"No, he will spend a while in communication, what you call prayer. After we have had tea you can take him in a cup of tea and have a chat."

A breeze was rustling the mosquito netting as Mrs Wilson offered the plate of bread and butter around the table. Arthur took two slices and some jam.

"How long have you been out here, Mr Wilson?"

"About fifteen years. I was out here as a child, my parents managed a plantation, but we went home when my father died. Gladys," he smiled at Mrs Wilson, "and I got married during the depression. I could not get work of any sort, so I wrote to the Company that had employed dad, said I knew a lot more about running a tea plantation than I did, anyway, they offered us this place and we've been here ever since; haven't even been home for a holiday."

Mrs Wilson laid her hand on her husband's arm, "the best thing that ever happened to us, wasn't it, Fred? If we hadn't come here we wouldn't have had the privilege of knowing Frank."

Arthur bit into the bread and jam sandwich and took a cup of boiling tea from Mrs Wilson.

"Thank you, what about the storm Mr Wilson? I was told it was strange, unnatural,frightening

Yes, it was almost a year ago, the storm clouds had been gathering all day. It was dark, almost like night, the pickers had stopped work, they were scared, there was something in the air, electricity, I suppose, we could all feel it. I sent Frank out to see if there was anybody still working and to bring them in. I went out myself in a different direction, the pickers live in a camp down the road, but they were starting to gather in front of the bungalow as we left, they were scared.

I'd been out for about an hour, I'd found nobody and I started to make my way back. As you can see the plantations are in the hills, the bushes are planted on tiers to trap the rain just like the vineyards.

I was on the North hill, when I thought I saw Frank across the valley on a lower hill. I shouted to him and waved my arms. Just then the storm broke, a great flash of forked lightning came out of the sky and hit the hill where Frank was; at the same time a peal of thunder broke almost over my head, I've never heard anything like it. We get plenty of storms here, bad ones, but this was different, I was really frightened, the earth vibrating and shaking. I started to run down the north hill towards Frank and the sky opened up, the rain came down like a dam had broken, it was a river of water, the earth turned into mud. I could hardly walk, it took me at least an hour to get to the spot where I'd seen Frank, when I got there, there was no sign of him, the ground was all black and burned from the lightning, the bushes were burned, everything was dead. I looked for Frank for a long time, but he wasn't there, then I started home, I don't know how long it took me, it was like walking up a stream, through a swollen river. Frank wasn't in the bungalow; nobody had seen him. Most of the pickers spent that night nearby, the others camped around where they could. At first light I went out with some of them to look for Frank again, it had stopped raining by then, there was a lovely sunrise, it was a fine morning, it's like that here a country full of extremes.

I went up to the burning hill alone, we've called it that since then. As the sun rose, and steam was rising gently from the earth, but it was still very wet, there was no sign of Frank up there: there was nothing, the whole hill had been burned by the lightning, everything was dead; there was a terrible smell of burning in the air. I left the burning hill and started down towards the valley. When I was about halfway down I saw a body lying at the bottom; it had to be Frank, I started to run down the hill and slipped, I rolled down slipping and sliding in the mud and landed by the body. I was winded and lay there in the mud looking at it, I remember how quiet it was, the body was face down in a stream made by the rain, there was blood coming from it and mixing with the rainwater stream. I got up and turned the body over, it was horrible, the face was almost completely gone, torn away, and there were terrible marks on his arms and chest. I was so shocked I didn't know what to do, I just sank on my knees in the mud looking at the body. One of the pickers found us later, I don't know how long it was; he ran back to the bungalow to get help. I somehow forced myself to pick up the body and started back. The pickers came to meet me, but I couldn't let them touch him, they fell in behind me, everyone was silent. It's hard to tell you what happened next. I still find it hard to believe, it was like a dream, the steam was rising from the ground and everything was so silent, so quiet. We came up the lower road to the clearing, as we started across it I looked up, and there he stopped talking for a moment and put his hand to his eyes, as if he were going to cry, and there on the veranda was Frank, looking at me.

Mr Wilson was almost choking now, he came down the steps and walked towards me. I didn't know what to do, I was frightened, shocked, I don't know. He walked across the clearing towards me, I knew there was something wrong, something different, he didn't look quite the same. He walked differently, he walked slowly, awkwardly, he was pale and thin. He walked up to me, I was alone then, the pickers had run away. He stepped in front of me and said, "Don't weep, old man." Then he put his hands on the body and said. "This boy is happy now, he is with my Father," then he walked to the veranda. I put the body down there, I could not speak, I didn't know what to say.

Mrs Wilson came out of the kitchen then, when she saw him she fell on her knees and prayed. He knelt and prayed with her, he told her he was the Son of God and that we should not be afraid. I didn't know what to think, when someone tells you that they are the Son of God, you would normally think that they were off their head, but with everything that had happened throughout that strange night, I didn't know what to believe. But he was different, he looked the same, but he was different all right. But then if God chooses your body to put his son's soul into you would be different.

The boy settled into life at the plantation, and although he looked like Frank I knew he wasn't our Frank any more he was peaceful and quiet, but spent a lot of time meditating, talking with seers and the gurus that passed through the plantation but still lead a pretty normal life, but he took an interest in the less fortunate of life and the sick and lame.

Some weeks passed. Frank got quieter and quieter, mediated more, spent time in prayer, then the miracles started, he had healed a man's withered arm; he brought the a plantation workers husband back from the dead, and many others, but he did these things quietly and without trying to bring attention to himself, we only found out about them when we were told by the plantation workers what he had done, and all the time more and more people started arriving, and pretty soon each morning when we awoke there was a sizeable crowd outside the bungalow each morning, we let the plantation go then, couldn't get the pickers to work anyway. I expect we will get kicked out soon, but we are not worried, we will go with him."

"Who was the dead boy, Mr Wilson?"

"I don't know, nobody knew, you get a lot of drifters coming to the plantation, they work for a few days, then move on. I suppose he was one of them. It's funny, but he really did look like a bit like Frank, we got boys up here to bury him. We assumed that a tiger had killed the lad, of course there were no tracks, what with the rain, it's odd really because there had been no reports of Tigers in the area for years."

Just then the door opened and Mrs Wilson came in and set another pot of tea on the table.

"Frank will see you now, Mr Green, would you like to take him in a cup of tea, he's in there," she pointed to a door in the corner of the room.

Arthur took the cup of tea and went to the door and knocked. Frank was standing by the window looking out at the crowd gathering outside. He turned to greet Arthur, and once again Arthur had the feeling of recognition, just for a second.

Frank was standing when I entered the room,

"Mr Green I am pleased to meet you." He took the cup of tea, and we shook hands. "You can see that I am a product of English foster parents by the amount of tea I drink." He smiled and sat down at a table and motioned me to sit opposite.

"You are a journalist, Mr Green, and I understand that you have been sent here to see if what the people say of me is true. I understand," he said reassuringly, "I won't be offended, it is something I must get used to. I expect you would like to take notes, please feel free to."

Arthur took a notebook and pen from his pocket and set them on the table.

Frank smiled "I will drink my tea while we talk."

Arthur looked into his eyes and tried to find, he wasn't sure what, humour, over confidence, a flaw, a mistake, a hint of something that would sow the seeds of doubt in him. There was nothing except a quiet peaceful confidence. Arthur picked up his pen. "Frank, may I call you Frank?"

"I have no other name."

"Frank who was Jesus?"

"Jesus is my Brother."

"You know him?"

"No, I was apart from everyone, in preparation for my visit to the earth."

"Who prepared you?"

"My Father."

"And you came from Heaven?"

"Yes."

"What is Heaven like?"

"Heaven is everything but the earth."

"Could you see the earth?"

"Sometimes my Father brought me near so that I could see where my work lay."

"Jesus was born and raised on the earth, why weren't you?"

"My task is greater than my brothers', there is not so much time."

"Why isn't there so much time?"

"A great war has just finished. If another war comes my Father will be done with the earth, he has sent me to avert it.to bring peace"

"How were you prepared for your visit to the earth?"

"I was taught the customs and languages of man."

"Were you always in the form of man?"

"For as long as I can remember."

"What form did God; your Father take?"

"When I saw Him, he was as man."

"How long did your preparation last?"

"I don't know. There is no time as on earth."

"Why did your Father choose India for your visit?"

"He said that India needed me more than any country."

"What other languages do you speak?"

"French, German, Spanish, Russian and Chinese."

"How did you actually get to the earth?"

"I don't know. My Father said my training must end, that I was needed here. I slept and when I awoke I was here."

"That was the night of the storm?"

"Yes."

"Do you remember the storm?"

"No."

"And when you awoke you were here?"

"On a path near the plantation. I followed the path and came to the bungalow. When Mrs Wilson saw me she called me Frank; that has been my name since then."

"If your work lies throughout the world, why have you stayed here for a year?"

"I found that by men's standards that I was physically weak. I have stayed here to gain strength. My work will be long and hard, I must be strong, but I will leave here soon, I am nearly ready now."

"Has your Father spoken to you since you came to the earth?"

"Yes, we can communicate through prayer."

Arthur looked up quickly into the deep brown eyes.

"Frank, I think you are a bloody liar, a crook, a con man."

There was no movement in the eyes. He put his hand on Arthur's arm. "I understand your doubt, Mr Green, it is human, but in spite of it I shall do my work. Now if you will excuse me I must rest, I am still not as strong as I should be."

Arthur put the book in his pocket, left the table and went to the door; he stopped and turned. "Frank, I didn't mean what I said about you being a liar and that, but I had to say it."

Frank smiled at him, "I know, Mr Green, I know."

Arthur turned and left the room.

Mr & Mrs Wilson looked up expectantly at Arthur. Mr Wilson was lighting his pipe, between puffs he said. "Well, what do you think of our boy, Mr Green?"

"I can honestly say Mr Wilson, that I have never experienced anything like this evening. He seems genuine, he is a remarkable boy, I feel honoured to have been here."

Mr Wilson got up, "We are glad that they sent someone as understanding as you Mr Green."

Arthur was looking around the room everything seemed so ordinary the furniture, the paintings on the wall, the sideboard with the "best china on display Mrs Wilson interrupted his thoughts "Rhani said she would wait outside for you, Mr Green."

Mr Wilson got up and said, "We've grown very fond of Rhani, Mr Green, and it's plain to us that she thinks a lot of you, but I hope you realise that the great love of her life is India; she believes that through Frank India and her brothers estate will thrive again,be reborn."

Arthur looked at him, "I realise that Mr Wilson. but I hadn't intended to compete, not on an international level anyway he said with a smile." He held out his hand and said, "I hope I may come again. If I am to be the herald of the new Son of God I shall need a lot more information."

Mr Wilson took his hand and said, "As long as you tell the truth, Mr Green, you will always be welcome."

Arthur said, "I hope Frank feels that way too, Mr Wilson," and went out onto the veranda.

It was dusk now, there were several fires still burning in the clearing, the flames twinkled in the twilight, and the still night air was filled with drifting smoke. He stood on the veranda, letting his eyes get accustomed to the darkness. There were groups of people around the fires, they were just sitting and talking, and waiting. He wondered where they were from.

From almost the beginning of time India had been full of religious sects and cults, he wondered what made these people think that the Indian boy with an English name was worth sitting and waiting in the dust for. Most of them probably knew nothing of the miracles, but they had come here just the same, maybe the first decuples were here, if he was to have any.

He started to think how he would write the story. It would be hard to convince people, but first he had to convince himself. In the light of the fires he saw Rhani waving to him. He went down the steps and walked across the clearing to her. She was sitting by the fire talking to Achmed and Ravi, he sat down with them. They were silent for a while, and Rhani said, "You look pale, Arthur, what happened?"

"Nothing happened, I just feel pale, that's all. We talked, I asked him some question and then I left."

"What do you think?"

"It isn't what I think that counts, I must have proof. I must see the man with the withered arm, and the man that died; what I think doesn't count."

"It does to me, Arthur."

Arthur looked across the fire at Rhani, the firelight was dancing on her face. She looked so beautiful, he realised that he was falling in love with her.

He seems like an honest and genuine young man in fact remarkable but that doesn't mean I believe, "I think that he is a most remarkable young man. He is gentle and understanding, kind," he paused, "Rhani, I must have proof, I'm sorry but I'm made that way, that's the way I am, perhaps my job has made me like it, maybe in centuries to come I'll be known as doubting Arthur." He smiled, trying to make her smile too, but she didn't smile, she just looked into the fire.

After a while Achmed and Ravi got up and went to the car. Arthur got up and walked around the fire and sat next to Rhani and put his arm around her. "Rhani, it is very important to me that I am honest with, you, right now it is the most important thing in the world, but you wouldn't want me to lie to you, would you?" He took her hand, "that would be no way to start a beautiful friendship, would it?"

She looked up at him and said, No" doubting Arthur", no way at all," and smiled. They got up and walked to the car.

The lights on the old Mercedes had long ceased to function. They pulled away from clearing onto the lower road slowly, there were still some stragglers arriving. The moon had risen and was bright as they came to an old bridge. Arthur looked out of the window and said, "Is that a river? I didn't notice it before."

"Yes," said Rhani, there is not much of it at any time except during the monsoon. The wild animals come to drink, there are often Water Buffalo here."

Arthur said, "could we see if they are there now?"

Rhani told Achmed to stop the car and they got out and walked back to the old stone bridge. Below them were half a dozen Water Buffalo standing in the stream, Rhani leant on the bridge and looked down into the muddy water. "If you stand by a water hole for a week,

Arthur, you will see every living creature in India, from an Elephant to a flea."

"Would you see a Tiger?"

"You would, yes, but not in this area."

"Where would you see them?"

"To the West, in the mountains of Nepal, or to the North in the Punjab. There was a boy killed by one."

"Here?"

"I don't know, when they hunt they cover vast areas, a stray one could have wandered down here, but it didn't eat the boy."

"Surely it would have killed other people or animals to live. Were there reports of other attacks?"

"No."

"Doesn't that seem strange to you?

Strange ? maybe, but it is all so strange. Everything is strange.

It is strange that God should send another son to the earth after2000 years.

"Yes, but the Tiger isn't the Son of God, it has to eat.

I don't know the answer Arthur, but I do know there is nothing false about the boy, I feel it deep inside, I am as certain of him as I am of anything."

Arthur looked at the great strange beasts with drooping horns, they stared back at him like statues, after a minute he said, "I feel it too. The boy has an aura of goodness that hangs about him, a belief in himself that cannot be mistaken."

She looked up at him excitedly, her eyes shining in the moonlight, her white teeth flashed; she threw her arms around him laughing happily

.Oh Arthur I knew you would believe.

He pulled her close to him, this laughing eager child. He felt the warmth of her, the shape of her body under the sari, and he pulled her head to his and kissed her, hard. She responded fiercely, almost aggressively, when they had finished kissing he held her, absorbing the feel of her and the smell of her hair like a blind man. Then the Buffaloes watched as they walked hand in hand to the car and Rhani said, "Tomorrow you shall meet the man who had the withered arm" and you will see.

Achmed started the car and drove slowly down the dusty track by the light of the moon.

The Imperial was in darkness when they arrived and they stood on the steps shouting their goodnights to Achmed and Ravi, like revellers after a party, their voices echoing around the empty square. The sound of the old car faded into the night until there was nothing

They went into the old hotel, and fumbled for matches on the old desk,

Arthur lit an oil lamp and its gentle light ran down the hall. He took Rhani's hand and led her into the Bar, "we must celebrate. Do you have any champagne?"

"Yes, but should we celebrate the coming of God's Son with champagne?" she laughed.

He looked into her eyes and said, "It's us I want to celebrate, it's us."

Rhani went through a door behind the Bar as Arthur struck a match and lit an oil lamp. By the lamp was a faded photograph of the Hotel staff taken on the front steps. Charley stood by Jahmel, behind them was lots of white coated boys, all smiling with their arms folded. As Rhani came back carrying a dusty bottle, Arthur said, "When was that taken?"

She put the bottle on the counter and walked across the room and took the photograph from the wall and looked at the back. "Fifteen years ago."

"Is the man with the withered arm there?"

She studied the photograph. "No, Majid is not here, but he worked here then."

"Yes", Arthur walked behind the bar and took down two glasses from the shelf, then popped the cork from the champagne. It hit the curtain and before it reached the floor the champagne was bubbling over the bar, we won't mind if it is warm will we? he filled the glasses and took them to where Rhani stood. He raised his glass in 'a toast to us.' They finished the wine and Arthur turned out the lamp, and they left the bar arm in arm. At the top of the stairs Rhani left him and went to her room without a word.

Arthur pulled back the curtains in his room and a shaft of moonlight cut through the darkness. He undressed and got into bed.

He lay there unable to sleep, he thought of the bridge, how Rhani had clung to him, the way her body felt against his. He opened his eyes with a start; there standing in the moonlight by his bed Rhani stood, the moonlight making her a silhouette

Arthur was awake early the next morning but Rhani had gone. He lay thinking of how she had come to him and given herself completely, a natural act of love, he was even more sure that he loved her. When the room grew lighter he got up and went to the heavy wardrobe and took down his bag and took out a large note book and pen and got back into bed and started to write.

"Today in the dusty plains of another world that is called India, I met the second Son of God. A boy with dark skin and long black hair and a face that could only be described as beautiful, who moves and looks like any one of us, but who has an aura of goodness and love that cannot be mistaken. As I write the pilgrims are starting to arrive at his home, the Plantation of the Rising Moon. The pilgrims from the surrounding areas where word of mouth had carried the news, by the time that you read this, pilgrims from all over the country will be arriving at the disused plantation. The boy was brought to the earth nearly a year ago during a violent storm that started the monsoon season and was taken into the house of the middle aged English couple who manage the plantation. They have since given up their work and dedicated their lives to caring for him .. I have spoken to him of his preparation; he knows the major languages of the earth and seems ready for the task ahead of him, but the fact that he was physically weak when he arrived, suggests that his training was not complete. He says that a second world war has angered his father and that if the violence and bloodshed does not stop his Father will end the world.

He preaches against the use of Temples and Churches and against organised religion; he says that people should adopt their own standards and moral code of behaviour. Tomorrow I am to meet Majid, a man that he healed of a withered arm, and a plantation worker that he brought back from the dead. He will soon be ready to start his work and will travel the world bringing unity and peace. If this slim boy can succeed in his gigantic task the troubles of the world may soon be over. He says that Heaven is everything but the earth. A world with people that believe in one God may soon extend its boundaries."

Sleep overtook Arthur, and when he woke again looked at the paper he had written at early light and wondered what Bill Steel the arch cynic would think of it and the Fleet street hacks when Arthur awoke again the room was bright with sunlight and Charley was standing by the bed with a cup of tea.

"Good morning, Mr. Green. Miss Rhani says that she will have breakfast in half-an-hour."

"Good morning, Charley." Arthur took the tea; "Charley did you know Majid?"

"Of course, sir, he worked here until recently, but now he has gone to the plantation to Frank."

"Isn't it unusual that a man with one arm should work here?"

"Yes, sir, but Jahmel brought him to me personally, and said that a place should be found for him. He worked in the kitchen. and did odd jobs"

"What do you know about Frank? They say that he is the Son of God. Have you seen him?"

"No, sir, I'm not interested in religion, I believe that it has done my country much harm."

"But he wants to do away with religion, organised religion anyway."

"Then perhaps I will like him after all, I will run your bath now, sir."

When Charley was in the bathroom Arthur put the notebook back in his bag. The street noises were starting to get louder as Arthur went into the bathroom. Charley was arranging the towels by the side of the bath. Charley looked up as he came into the room.

"It's funny that you should mention Majid, sir, because I was very surprised when he left, he had such an easy life here, and he always had a little money, even when we stopped getting wages, he had money. I thought he must be stealing food and selling it. If he was, he was very clever, because I could never catch him, I tried, but I never could. Jahmel always treated him better than the others, gave him the easy jobs and that sort of thing.

""Well, he only had one arm"

"Yes, sir, I suppose that was it." Charley put his hand in the water, "there I think you will find that just right, sir, if there is nothing else I can do, Jahmel will be back today and there is plenty to do."

Rhani was waiting for Arthur when he came down stairs, she was wearing a white sari and had her hair piled upon her head in the western style. She took his hand and he bent to kiss her, but she turned away and said, "Arthur there are things that we must talk about before Jahmal returns. She walked through the open door and onto the steps of the Hotel, Arthur followed.

"Arthur you must say nothing of last night or our feelings for each other to Jahmel. I think that he will be unhappy when he returns from Delhi and I don't want to add to his troubles."

"Why do you think that he will be unhappy? Because of the Mughal's?

"It is a feeling I have, my brother and I are very close., I can feel it. If I tell him of our feelings it will only add to his problems, I will find time to tell him, Frank will leave soon and things will be back to normal. I will tell him then."

"But that may be weeks, you know I cannot stay till then, I will have to go back to London."

"But surely you will stay with Frank now. You can travel with him and send articles on his progress."

"Maybe, it depends on my boss, but even then I would be away from you."

"Not if I followed Frank too. I believe it will be many years before he leaves India, that way we could be together. But anyway we must not say anything now, I know Jahmel, he will not agree to anything when he is unhappy, when he is happy I can have my way.

I will see if the breakfast is ready." She went back into the Hotel.

The small square was starting to fill up now, the traders were sitting cross legged beside their fruit and vegetables spread on the ground, and the bartering was beginning. Arthur saw the beggar boy in the corner of the square looking at him, he smiled at him and the boy smiled back. Not much use in waving thought Arthur and turned and walked into the Imperial.

Rhani was already seated at the table when Arthur went into the dining room, a large plate of toast was on the table. Arthur sat down and she poured himself a cup of tea, and said, "we will see Frank again this morning, we will go after breakfast. When you have seen Majid, will you send news of Frank to your paper?"

"If I am convinced. You must understand Rhani that to make people believe in Frank I must have proof. The people who read my story won't have met him, they will only believe if I believe.

"They will believe the World News; they will believe what you tell them

"No, even with proof it will be hard enough to make them believe."

"But while you are waiting another reporter may come here and write the story, a reporter who may not be so concerned with proof."

"Yes, that may be so, but we will see Majid today, he may convince you.

Rhani pushed back her chair and stood up. "Then we shall go now" Doubting Arthur," I will send word to Achmed." She left the room and Arthur poured himself another cup of tea.

They were still sitting in the dining room when Achmed came in, he was smiling and held his hat in his hand. "We go plantation, yes?"

Rhani said, "Yes, Achmed, you wait outside we will be out soon."

Arthur took Rhani's hand as she left the table. "When I go to Delhi to send the story, will you come with me?"

Rhani looked into his eyes and said, "if I went to Delhi with you, Arthur, I could never come back, Jahmel would not allow it unless we were married, and you are already married."

They left the dining room in silence, and walked out into the bright sunlight and got into the old Mercedes. As they pulled out of the square I looked at the little beggar boy. He saw me and smiled, I felt guilty, even if Frank wasn't the Son of God, he could help the boy, and the other boys like him. How long should the truth matter, if a lie would help the boy, wouldn't it be better to lie than to tell the truth and let fathers' go on maiming their children. The journey seemed longer although, everything was the same, groups of people still walked the dusty road, others were camped by the roadside, cooking with old corned beef tins, the spindly smoke from their fires drifting across the road. Farm workers were bending in the fields; Oxon were pulling stone wheels that crushed the grain. The water Buffalo were standing below the stone bridge in the stream, but it seemed longer, maybe because Rhani and I were sitting apart in the back of the car, last night she had lent against me and the breeze from the window had blown her hair in my face. Once Achmed stopped the car and helped push a cart with a broken wheel off the road. When we were alone I thought Rhani might say something, anything, but she didn't speak and I didn't know what to say.

The plantation hills rose out of the plain ahead and we soon bumped our way past the faded board and onto the lower road up into the hill to the clearing in front of the bungalow. There were more people than before sitting and waiting around their little fires. Mr and Mrs Wilson were moving among them with food and water. They waved when they saw us, and we edged our way through the crowd towards them.

Mrs Wilson looked up from her knees and said, "Frank's not here." She was bathing the head of a small child with a damp cloth. "Too much travelling and not enough food, that's the matter with this little mite, she'll be all right when she has rested. Perhaps you'd ask them to move her into the shade, Rhani."

Rhani spoke to the people, and the child and they carried the baby to a Mango tree and laid her beneath it.

"He's been gone since dawn," said Mrs. Wilson, wiping her hands on a grubby apron.

"Where has he gone to?"

"To a village on the other side of the hill. There's a dispute over a water hole between two families of the village. We heard last night that one man had been killed already." She looked at me, "Water is more precious than money out here, Mr Green." She looked up into the cloudless sky. "It'll be a good thing when the monsoons come, we are very short of water now."

"Mrs Wilson I want to see Majid."

"Majid is with Frank, Mr Green."

Rhani said, "when will Frank be back, Mrs Wilson?"

"Late today I expect. He goes further each day. He has told us that if we are to go with him we must get ready. I think we shall leave soon and he will start his work."

Rhani looked around and said, "is there anything we can do to help, Mrs Wilson?"

"No dear, thank you, we give them a little bread and water and make them as comfortable as we can. They will wait for Frank, till he speaks to them then they will be happy if he he blesses them; but they'll be happy to have seen him. You will hear when he returns, you must come back then."

As we started back towards the car I saw Mr Wilson carrying another small child to the shade of the tree.

On the side of the hill bushes had been pulled out and clearings made for the crowds that were still arriving, they squatted in the dust and waited. The road was more crowded as we started back to the Imperial, people carrying children, pushing and pulling homemade carts, some hanging on to ox drawn wagons, or riding old bicycles piled high with their belongings.

When we eventually pulled up outside the Imperial Achmed spoke to Rhani, he looked sad and spoke quietly,. Rhani nodded and we got out. As we walked up the steps Rhani said, "he doesn't want to go there any more, he says that soon it will be pointless to go in the car, it will be impossible to drive on the road." She stopped suddenly at the top of the steps. "Jahmel is back."

"How do you know?"

"I can feel it, I know."

We went into the Hotel, it was still morning and the curtains hadn't been drawn yet.

Jahmel was sitting in the Bar, a bottle of whisky was on the counter. He looked up when we came in and spoke to Rhani, he didn't even look at me. Rhani said something to him, then turned to me and said, "you had better leave us, Arthur, there are family matters that we have to discuss.

As I went upstairs I could hear Jahmels voice. I lifted the mosquito net and got onto the four-poster. I closed my eyes and listened to the sounds of the market below drifting through the open window; the shouts of the traders, bicycles clicking by, and wheels creaking over the bumpy stones

I awoke suddenly, the silence was overpowering, I looked at my watch, it had stopped, it was the first time I had looked at my watch since I'd been in India. I lifted the mosquito net and went to the window, the square was deserted except for the beggar boy, it was evening and the sun had gone behind the mud huts. I went to the bathroom and splashed cold water on my face and went downstairs. Charley was in the Bar polishing glasses, he smiled when he saw me.

"Good evening, Mr Green, did you have a good sleep? I looked in on you a couple of hours ago, but Miss Rhani said not to wake you. Would you like a drink, sir?"

I said a pot of tea would be very welcome, and did he know where Jahmel and Rhani were?

"They've gone out, sir, they've been gone about an hour." He returned with the tea and said, "Is there anything else I can get you?"

"No thank you, Charley, the tea is all I need." I was drinking the tea and wondering what the raised voices had been about.

I looked into the mirror behind the bar and saw Jahmel come into the room. Before I had a chance to turn he was slapping me on the back, "Arthur dear boy, I'm afraid we've been neglecting you, but they said you were sleeping and I did not want to disturb you." He sat on the bar stool beside me, "did you have a good day?"

"Not really, we went to the plantation to see Majid but he had gone with Frank to settle a village dispute."

Jahmel asked Charley for a scotch and water then said, "never mind you will see him soon." He took an envelope from his inside pocket and handed it to me. "Your fame has spread, Arthur, some acquaintances of mine wish to see you in Delhi."

I put down my drink and opened the letter. It was printed on fine paper and had a gold embossed crest in one corner. Across the top of the sheet in raised black old English lettering it said, 'The Colonial Club', Chandni Chauk, Old Delhi.

"Dear Mr Green,
It is with a great sense of honour that I have learned that such a notable member of the journalistic profession is in the area. I would be pleased; it would give me great pleasure if you would be the guest of myself and my friends at the Colonial Club. We have news that is of vital importance to your country and ours."

The letter was signed Jennah Ghatt, Minister.

When I had finished reading the letter Jahmel said. "It is only fair that I tell you, Arthur, these men are very powerful, it is best that you go."

I finished my drink and said, "I don't care how powerful they are, I am not going anywhere until I've seen Majid."

Jahmel looked at me for a minute and said, "Look, Arthur, you don't think I would have gone if I'd any choice, do you? You know as well as I do there are British soldiers being murdered every day on the streets of Bombay, Calcutta, Delhi, all across India. The Mughal are responsible for half these deaths, they organise the riots, they are everywhere. Government Ministers, lawyers, business men, they're in the schools. The Civil Service, even the Police; knowing my feelings towards the British, do you think I would have anything to do with them if I had a choice?"

"If you feel like that, why did you go?"

"I can't explain, Arthur, perhaps one day you will understand." Jahmel went behind the bar and took a bottle of scotch from the shelf and filled his glass, he drained his glass and filled it again. "You will go, Arthur, and when you do go for God's sake be careful, agree to what they say, if you don't, you'd better leave India." He drained his glass again and left the bar.

Charley came back through the door behind the bar and started polishing glasses again. I took the bottle from the bar and filled a glass.

"Charley, what do you know about the Mughal?"

He didn't answer.

I asked again.

"It is better not to talk of them, sir."

I banged my empty glass down on the counter. "What the bloody hell is going on? first Jahmel tells me I must agree to whatever they say, and now you won't even talk about them."

Charley carried on polishing the glasses. "You should understand, sir that this is India. The ways of India and the Indians are very strange, you could live here all your life and not understand. Indians believe in the impossible and often see it. Men climbing ropes that disappear into the sky, walking on red hot coals, sleeping on nails.

Men do these things, strange men, because they believe that they can. The Mughal tell the people that they will end the drought and famine, that everyone will be educated and live well, like human beings; the people believe them. The Western World has lost the power of belief, the extent of their belief is that if they use a certain toothpaste their teeth will be whiter. It is said that faith, and faith is pure belief, can move mountains, in India sir it happens."

Rhani came in as Charley started on another glass. She looked cool and distant as if we hadn't been properly introduced and wasn't sure if she should be so forward as to speak to me. "Arthur, Jahmel says that would you please not be late for dinner. He says he has an announcement to make." Having delivered her speech, she turned and left the room.

I got off my stool, the scotch had relaxed me, as I was leaving the room I said, "I'm sorry I shouted, Charley."

"That's all right, sir, it's the heat I expect."

I lay on the bed and smoked a cigarette, what on earth could the Mughal want with me, or Jahmel for that matter? There was a knock on the door and a houseboy came in, he went to the bathroom and started to run the bath. I got up and went to the window, the square was empty again, except for the little beggar boy, he sat in the corner in the shadows and looked at the Hotel as a wind swirled the dust around him. When the houseboy had left the room I undressed and went down the steps into the bath and lay in the cool water; something must happen soon. I must go to Delhi and send the story, or go home. I got out of the bath and dried myself and walked back into the bedroom. The Major's uniform was laid out on the bed with a clean shirt; the boots were polished again. I got dressed and went downstairs. Jahmel heard me and came out of the bar. "Arthur, let's have a quick one before we eat." He was obviously in a drinking mood, he was just starting to tell me about Pinky Wilson's Bentley again when the dinner gong sounded and we finished our drinks and went into the dining room. Rhani was putting a small posy of flowers on the table, she smiled when she saw us.and we joined her at the table, they were both smiling and seemed in a better mood now.

Jahmel opened a bottle of wine and filled our glasses, and we stood up. "Now I have a pleasant task to perform," he looked at Rhani.

"Now I'm sure you will remember, my dear when you were a little girl, the parties we used to have for the guests at the start of the monsoon." He looked at me now. "In the old days, Arthur when the Hotel was always full we used to have a party to welcome the monsoon, it was more of a carnival really. The people in the town used to organise a procession and roast an ox in the evening, and we would have a grand dinner and ball at the Hotel for the guests, we called it the Rain Feast. I have decided that this year we shall revive the custom and hold it next Saturday week, that gives us nearly two weeks to prepare. I shall invite the most important people in the area," he raised his glass and Rhani and I stood up, we all raised our glasses and drank to the Rain Feast. As we sat down Jahmel said, "it used to be very grand in the old days, Arthur, we even had people come down from Delhi, good publicity for the Hotel you know." He was excited now, "Rhani you must make a list of who we would like, what about music? we used to have a small band in the old days, you haven't seen the ballroom have you, Arthur? It's not a ballroom really, just an extension we had built across the back of the hotel, but there is a stage and the floor is quite good. We even had one of those great balls with faceted glass on it, it hangs in the centre of the ceiling and reflects the light, it is supposed to turn really, but we will have to wait until we get electricity for that. of course, but the candles and oil lamps make it sparkle Arthur as you're going to Delhi, if I give you a couple of addresses perhaps you could arrange the band; nothing too grand you know, as long as it's music to dance to. I'll speak to some of the shopkeeper's and townspeople tomorrow, it'll be good for the town,.good for all of us.

He paused for breath, and I said, "what about clothes, Rhani? perhaps you'd like to come to Delhi with me and buy a new outfit."

Jahmel burst out laughing, "not necessary, old boy, fancy dress, fancy dress, that'll be your job tomorrow, Rhani, sorting out the fancy dress." And that was the end of my idea.

The houseboys came bustling in with trays, as I said, "you've forgotten one thing Jahmel, I'm not sure if I'll be going to Delhi yet."

Jahmel didn't think that was worth commenting on and said, "it will be just like old times, the start of a new life for the Imperial. I must see how the wine situation is, should have champagne really, but

I'm afraid we can't run to that, they drink like fish at these do's' you know."

The houseboys had finished serving now and they left the room and we started to eat. Between mouthfuls Jahmel said, "good that's settled then, I shall enjoy organising it. What do you think of the idea, Rhani?"

She looked at me and said, "I'm sure it will be wonderful, I hope Arthur will be here to enjoy it."

Jahmel put down his knife and fork, "Arthur, of course he'll be here, won't you, Arthur?"

"I don't know, when I do go to Delhi, I'll have to cable the paper either with the story or to say I'm coming home."

Jahmel looked shocked, "what do you mean, go home, you've seen Frank haven't you? of course you'll send the story, where's the problem?"

I picked up my glass of wine and looked at it, "the problem is, Jahmel, that I've seen him, I got to convince the readers of the World News that a second Son of God is living here and now, and until I've seen Majid I don't think I can do that, that's the problem."

Jahmel got up and got the decanter of brandy from the dresser and came back to the table and poured himself a glass and drank it. He looked at me, he looked weak and tired. "Arthur, you don't realise how important it is to me that you send the story. You don't realise the work we've put into it, the hours I've spent with Frank, the work we have done. I must have visited every village within fifty miles of here, telling them of Frank, spreading the word." He straightened himself up, "I haven't even told Rhani yet, but while I was in Delhi I cabled the company that owns the plantation, and made them an offer for it, considering the state it's in I expect they will accept it."

Rhani jumped up, she looked furious, "you've done what? you must be mad, we can't even afford to run the Imperial, where do you think you will get the money?" She suddenly became aware of me again and sat down.

Jahmel leaned across the table towards her, "don't worry, Rhani, don't worry, I'm going to turn it into a monument to Frank. When the World knows of him people will flock here to see where he started his life on earth, the Imperial will be full again, we'll soon pay off the money, you'll see." He turned to me, "I was hoping to keep it as a surprise, Arthur, but you see now how important it is that you send the story, don't you?"

I wasn't sure if I was expected to reply so I kept quiet and started eating again

. So that was how he was going to fill the Imperial again, with Frank preparing to leave I wasn't sure how he would do it. He kept looking and I kept eating. He still kept looking. I said, "if I may use one of your horses I'll go to the plantation first thing tomorrow, Achmed won't drive there anymore, Majid may be back."

Jahmel looked relieved although Rhani still looked angry

I tried to bring her into the conversation abd said "What costume would you like to wear Rhani?" She looked at Jahmel and said, "I think perhaps Anne Bolyn, like her I think my days are numbered."

Jahmel laughed, "Women, Arthur they have no vision, no faith, it will be all right Rhani, the guests will be coming soon, and we will pay for the plantation in no time, you see it will be just like old times."

Rhani said, "Frank has been here for a year now and how many guests have we had? the money is nearly gone and you want to revive the Rain Feast."

Jahmel looked at her and said, "don't worry," he said it again more firmly, as if to end the discussion, "don't worry."

The houseboys came in with a tray of fresh fruit and a large pot of coffee. Nobody spoke until they left the room, then Rhani seemed to snap out of her angry mood and said, "We must invite the Wilsons'. Should we invite Frank?

Jahmel was peeling an orange, he looked up quickly, "of course, he won't come. I wouldn't invite him, he has more important things to do than go to parties."

Rhani said, "what would you like to wear, Arthur?"

"I don't know, I've never been to a fancy dress party, the kind of parties I go to I usually take a bottle of scotch with me, and hang on to it all night."

Jahmel said, "yes, well it won't be that sort of party, Arthur, but we'll find you something suitable to wear, you can organise all that Rhani." He filled my coffee cup and said, "you will try and organise some music while you are in Delhi, won't you?"

We drank our coffee and Jahmel got the brandy decanter from the Welsh dresser, and I thought if he puts a bill into the paper for all this, Bill Steel will pull his hair out, and we haven't even got to the Rain Feast yet.

We started to drink the brandy, Rhani, as usual wasn't included. After a couple of drinks Jahmel seemed to relax a little and started to sort out what each of us had to do. "So first thing tomorrow, Arthur you will go to the plantation and see Majid, then you will go to Delhi to meet Jennah Gatts and send your story; you will be back on Thursday or Friday and the Rain Feast will be on Saturday. Rhani you will write me a list of who we should invite, sort out the fancy dress and think about the catering, you will need some extra help in the kitchen, Charley will help you there, and I must prepare the guest list and organise the Towns people and the procession. Splendid, splendid, it'll be just fine."

Now that he had everything planned he seemed satisfied. "More brandy, Arthur?" I pushed my glass towards him. "Arthur, I'll let you into a little secret I think. I knew it would be you the paper sent out, I've been following your career with the World News very carefully, ever since you handled that avalanche story in Austria. I liked what you wrote, the way you wrote it, you showed a lot of real sympathy I could tell you wrote from the heart not like that fool Simon Johnson, the report he did on the Birmingham train crash sounded like a hospital report, no heart, no soul, no real feeling, just a factual report. No, I knew you were the man for this story, it had to be you, so I chose my time to send the story on Frank, I knew Simon Jenkins was in Switzerland covering the Bob Sleigh championships, so that left you, as senior reporter, I hope you don't mind, Arthur?"

"Why should I mind, it's a compliment, anyway it's nice to know somebody reads my reports." I finished my coffee, after Jahmel's confession things seemed to go a little flat, so I said, "I think I'll get some sleep now, perhaps you'd ask Charley to call me at first light and I'll get out to the plantation as early as possible."

Jahmel said he would, and I said goodnight and left the table.

I opened my eyes and there was Charley standing on the other side of the mosquito net holding a cup of tea. "Good morning, sir, did you sleep well?" He put the tea on the table beside the bed and went into the bathroom, I sipped the tea, it was hot and strong, the sound of the bath water came into the bedroom. Charley came to the door wiping his hands, "well, sir I hear that we'll be getting more guests at the Hotel soon."

I got out of bed and went to the window, "perhaps, Charley, it depends on what happens at the plantation today."

"Oh, I didn't mean that, sir, I meant the Rain Feast, I didn't answer.

Charley came to the window and stood beside me, we looked out together. Great spears of scarlet were wedging their way through the black sky, as the tip of the sun edged up over the village houses, the light was spreading it's way tentatively around the square; from a small alley to the right the small beggar boy squirmed his way through the dust to his spot in the corner. He had his bowl between his teeth, it made it look as if he was smiling, or was it grimacing. I felt a sadness in me that seemed to be centuries deep and I turned away from the window, I didn't want to see any more.

I went to the bathroom, Charley followed me in and turned off the bath taps and said, "that's funny isn't it, sir you were only talking about Majid the other day and I've just seen him outside."

I nearly fell into the bath, "what!" I rushed to the window, "where, where?" Charley was at the window now. "I don't see him now, sir, but he was there."

I rushed to the wardrobe and took a pound note from my jacket pocket and put it into Charley's top pocket. "Go and find him, Charley and bring him back here." I pushed him out into the hall and he ran off towards the stairs – I shouted, "don't come back without him." I ran back to the window, Charley ran down the steps of the Hotel into the square, and I got dressed.

A quarter of an hour later there was a knock at the door. Charley stood in the hall holding the arm of a small wiry Indian man of about forty. He pushed him into the room like he was handling me an umbrella, "this Majid, sir."

I said, "come in both of you, well done, Charley." Charley followed the little man into the room and closed the door. Majid looked frightened, and I said, "don't worry, Majid, I only want to ask you some questions."

Charley said, "I am afraid he doesn't speak English, sir."

I said, "that's odd, if he worked here for fifteen years why didn't Jahmel teach him, well never mind, perhaps you will translate

Charley." I signalled Majid to come further into the room and sit down, he sat on the edge of the chair and looked nervously at Charley. "Now, Charley tell him not to worry, that I only want to ask him some questions." Charley told him, but he still looked nervous. "Ask him to pull up the sleeves of his robe I want to look at his arms." Charley said a couple of words and took hold of his wrists and pulled back the robe to the shoulders. The left arm was a lot thinner than the right. "Ask him what happened to his arm," Charley spoke to him and pointed to the arm, he didn't answer. Charley spoke to him again and shook his left arm, he spoke to Charley quietly, he was still very nervous. "He says that it was damaged when he was a child."

"How was it damaged?"

"He says an Ox trod on him."

"And he couldn't use the arm from that time?"

"Yes."

"Then how is it that he can use it now?"

"He says that the arm was healed by the Messiah, Frank."

"Why did he go to Frank? what made him think that he could heal it?"

"Jahmel told him to go." I looked at the arm again it was very thin, but apart from that it looked all right. I held my arm up and wriggled my finger, and pointed to his arm, he did the same, his fingers worked too. "Ask him if he has a scar on the arm where the Ox stood on him."

"He says the scar vanished when the Messiah touched him."

I walked to the window and looked out, it was quite bright now. "Ask him what he is doing in town so early."

"He says that he has come to town to get provisions, the Messiah is going to an area that has Cholera, they are all going and they need medications and provisions." I took another pound note from my pocket and gave it to him. "Thank him for his help and tell him that I hope I haven't delayed him too much."

He left the room and Charley said, "if there is nothing else, sir I'll carry on." I was at the window again watching the beggar boy, I said, "thank you for your help Charley, and there is something else, if you see Achmed, tell him I'll need him, we are going to Delhi.

Chapter 4

I got undressed again and had my bath and shaved and then packed my bag, took it downstairs and left it in the hall. I opened the heavy front door and walked out onto the steps of the Hotel, it was still cool and empty, except for my friend in the corner, he was watching me. I went down the steps slowly and walked towards the boy, it felt like I was on a stage with a thousand of people watching me. When I got to him he gave me a Shirley Temple smile, a well-practiced smile, I felt awkward and didn't know what to say, so I said "Good morning," he didn't answer. I squatted down beside him wondering if he could speak, I looked around the square, his view of the square, still in the shade the Imperial loomed over everything, all was quiet, the little mud and bamboo houses that served as shops were shuttered. I looked at him again and said, "have you ever been to school?", he kept smiling and didn't answer. I was trying to think of some Indian words to try on him when he looked away from me at the lane that led to the plantation road, he looked back and still smiling said, "Achmed," he split the word into two syllables, and smiled even more at his effort. A moment later I heard the sound of the old Mercedes, it bumped into the square past us and stopped in front of the Imperial. Achmed got out and went into the Hotel and came out carrying my bag, put it into the back and got in the car to wait.

I turned to the boy and put my finger to my lips so that he should keep quiet, and tiptoed to the car, putting my hand through the open window onto Achmed's shoulder. He nearly fell out of the car with fright. I looked at the boy he was rolling from side to side laughing, then Achmed saw the boy and he laughed too. I went into the Hotel and thought well at least his day has started with a laugh. I went up the stairs and along the hall to Rhani's room and knocked. There was no reply so I went in, the room was a feminine version of mine. I moved quietly to the bed and lifted the mosquito net. Rhani was asleep, she looked like a child, her black silky hair across her face. I pulled the strands of hair aside and kissed her lightly, then went downstairs.

Charley was coming out of the bar and I said, "tell Rhani that I've gone to Delhi when she wakes, will you, Charley?"

I went down the steps of the Hotel and got into the front seat of the car and said, "don't worry, Achmed, we won't be stopping very much so I'll sit in the front this time. Achmed started the car and we were on our way. Leaving a cloud of exhaust fumes behind us

The roads were quite clear and we were away from Ranpure and onto the Delhi road quickly. It was a good road with a proper surface and we didn't meet much traffic until later in the morning, and then it was mostly old lorries heavily laden with cotton or tobacco. It was flat country farm land, and the workers were in the fields bending over their work, mainly women, they took no notice of the old car as it passed by so we smoked my cigarettes and drove in silence.

At about mid-day we stopped at a village in the shade of an old tree, the village was a smaller version of Ranpure. Achmed went to a house near an open fronted cafe and spoke to a bearded man, he came back carrying two large fuel cans and a funnel and filled the car with petrol. When he had finished he said that we would stop here until the sun was lower. I was glad to get out of the car, it was like a furnace in there, even with all the windows down.

Achmed returned the cans and we walked up the road to the cafe, there were a few rickety tables and chairs outside beneath a lattice work frame that was covered with a pink Bougainvillea. We sat at one of the tables, it was cooler in the shade and the sweet smell of the flowers filled the air. A waiter with a drooping moustache and beard and a dirty apron came out and spoke to Achmed. he nodded and said we will drink here only, Arthur, it is not good for eating, we will eat in Delhi. The waiter came back carrying a tray with four glasses on it and set them on the table. We had two glasses each, Achmed picked up one glass and sipped it, it was a dark brown in colour, and said, "cold tea, very good for hot weather." He picked up the other glass, it was light, more golden in colour, "Bagdi,, wheat whisky, very bad for hot weather," he roared out laughing at his joke and hit the table with his hand making the glasses jump. I took a sip from each glass, the cold tea was refreshing and the Bagdi was like vintage sulphuric acid, it felt like it was burning a new route to my stomach. We sat there amongst the flowers, drinking our tea,. Like Ranpure, everything stopped at midday and people fled from the sun, the village was very quiet.

After about half-an-hour three men came to the cafe and sat at a table near us, they ate curry and drank hot tea and talked quietly. Achmed spoke to them, but they did not answer him. There were several electric light bulbs hanging from the lattice work overhead and the electricity proved that we must be fairly near Delhi now. Achmed was fishing a small creature from my third glass of acid when we heard the rumbling sound of a heavy lorry approaching, the three men at the next table stopped talking and we all looked down the road towards the sound. It was a British Army lorry and it came slowly into the town in a cloud of dust. As it passed the cafe one of the men at the next table ran up the road and picked up a stone and threw it at the lorry. It hit the canvas side and bounced onto the road, he ran back into the cafe and shouted at Achmed and pointed at me, the two other men were standing now and shouting. Achmed shouted back and the man who had thrown the stone ran to the table and threw a punch at Achmed, he swayed back out of reach. As he swayed back he hit the man in the throat, he fell back into the dust choking and gasping for air, one of the other men at the table ran towards Achmed; as he came level with me I hit him with my left hand. He altered course slightly and stumbled through the open door of the cafe and hit the waiter who was coming out, they both fell into the tables and chairs inside, the other man said something and sat down.

Achmed said, "it is time to go, Baba Ji," as we walked to the car he said, "it is not right that we should pay the bill in a place that offers us no hospitality, is it, Sir?"

I said, "certainly not," and we ran to the car and left. As we left the village I said, "now that we are blood brothers, Achmed, I think it's time you called me Arthur, don't you?"

He looked very pleased and said, with a broad smile "yes, Arthur, I think that is a very good idea." After we had been driving for about half-an-hour he said, "When we get to Delhi I will stay with you, it is dangerous for an English man to be alone, there is a lot of ill-feeling towards the British, as you have seen. There are many people who want independence, the British to leave, they are important people, and the poor people look up to them and believe what they say."

I said, "you mean the Mughal Sect"?

"Yes, it is the Mughal but they are mostly in the cities, the country people know that their lives will not change whether the British are here or not."

Later that evening we entered the outskirts of Delhi. It was like the other villages at first, but then the houses grew thicker, and then roads had pavements, then there were glass fronted shops, and eventually the roads had pavements and tram lines.

The centre of old Delhi was surrounded by a high wall set amongst small houses, mostly brick built. The roads were full of people, they didn't seem to be going anywhere, they just walked around, there were groups of British troops standing around military vehicles. And standing on corners .. Nobody seemed to take much notice of us we stopped at the end of Chandni Chauk and Achmed said, "we must walk now, the Colonial Club is not far."

Chandni Chauk was a wide market street with stalls down the centre and openfronted windowless shops down each side. Achmed said, "it's very famous for silver and jewellery, Arthur, if you wish to buy something, tell me and I will buy it for you, they charge very high prices for foreigners especially thee British"

The stalls sold filigree work in silver and gold and at some of the stalls a man would be sitting making the jewellery with small pliers and soldering irons heated on open fires.. We carried on down the road until we came to the Colonial Club, it was a large white building with great marble columns each side of the entrance. We went up a couple of steps into the entrance hall, a thin man in a uniform was sitting at a desk writing. I went up to him and said, "Jennah Ghats," he looked up, "have you an appointment, sir?"

"I think so, he is expecting me, I expect he'll see me."

He stood up, "could I have your name, sir?"

I gave him my name,

he went through some swing doors at the end of the hall. Achmed said, "I have to see some relatives while I am in Delhi, I will come back in the morning. He turned to go, then stopped as if he had forgotten something and said, "if you should need me, Arthur, there is a jewellery shop near the car called the Annapurna Jewellery shop, ask for me there, they will know where I am," then he left the club, and walked back into the busy street

There were bench seats around the hall beneath the windows, and I walked to one and sat down, the sound of my steps on the marble floor echoed around the hall. A swing door opened and a small middle aged man came into the hall, he was wearing a very well cut dark blue suit with a gold albert across the waistcoat. He held out his hand when he saw me and walked across the hall smiling, "Mr. Green, how good of you to come," he put his arm around me and guided me back towards the swing door. "You will be my guest while you are in Delhi, Mr. Green, and you will want for nothing."

We went through the doors into a large room, it could have been a club in St. James's, there were leather armchairs and chesterfields of all shapes and sizes, there was a polished parquet floor with a large red and black carpet in the centre. The walls were covered with large gilt framed mirrors and oil paintings, over a columned fireplace was an oil painting of King George V1. everyone in the club was Indian except me, some were reading newspapers, others were sleeping or talking. He led me to the far side of the room to a group of four men, three were seated on a large chesterfield, and one in a large leather winged armchair, there were two empty chairs they stood up as we approached and Ghats said, "Gentlemen may I present Mr Arthur Green of World News. Mr Green, this is," he pointed to each man in turn and we shook hands, I caught, Minister of Internal Affairs and President of the North India Traction Company, and then we all sat down.

A white coated waiter came over, I ordered a scotch and added hopefully, ice,? the waiter left us and Jennah Ghats cleared his throat said, "what do you think of our club, Mr Green? It was built by the British many years ago then given to the Indian Government by your people here, they don't seem to think they'll be needing it much longer anyway."

I said, "it's very nice, but don't you find it a little English for your taste?"

He said that they found it very comfortable, but changes would be made in time, but after all it had been an English Club and they hoped to preserve it as such.as an object of architectural curiosity.

The waiter came back with the drinks and mine actually had ice in it, it was beautiful, Jennah Ghats said he would drink to a successful meeting and the others made appropriate noises. One of the men on the chesterfield, I think it was the President of the Traction Company said, "What do you think of the Messiah, Mr Green?"

Before I could answer Jennah Ghats said, "now, now, there will be plenty of time to talk, Mr Green must be tired after the journey, he must relax, we will give Mr Green some pleasant memories to take away from Delhi." He snapped his fingers at the waiter, who came back shortly with more drinks and took the empty glasses.

Jennah Ghats said, India, must seem very strange to you even alien Mr Green" the other side of the world, strange people and customs, a different culture" I am sure it is very strange for you

I said I thought it was very beautiful, but full of contrasts, and we all sat around like old friends making small talk for a while until Ghats looked at his watch and said, "it will soon be time for dinner, Mr Green, I will show you to your room." We all stood up and I said goodbye to the others and followed him from the room. We went through an archway at the far end of the room, up a flight of stairs and along a corridor. He opened a door and we went into a small lounge with a sofa and easy chair, a table and a desk, he pointed to another door and said "the bedroom is there, Mr Green, if there is anything you need just press that bell," and he pointed to the button on the wall. It was then that I realised I had left my bag in Achmed's car, I told Jennah Ghats and said that I would go and see if the car was still where I had left it. He said that it was not important and that only evening dress was worn at the club in the evening and he assumed I did not bring one, he was only waiting to see my size before sending one to me.

As he left the room he said, "dinner is at eight o'clock, Mr Green, we will see you later."

I went into the bedroom, there was a large bed, next to it on a table was a telephone, the first I had seen since I'd been in India, below the window was a dressing table. I went through another door into the bathroom and ran the bath and started to undress. I was about to get in when there was a knock on the door. I wrapped a towel around me and opened the door, a young girl stood outside, not more than fifteen years old. She had an evening suit and shirt over her arm, she was a very pretty girl and lightly tanned skin was contrasted by a simple white English style frock, her hair was long and black and nearly reached her waist. She held out the suit and said, "Minister Ghats told me to bring you this." She looked at my towel, it started to feel transparent, "and to see that you had whatever you wanted," she smiled, the meaning was explicit. I took the suit from her and she said, "my father was an English soldier, Minister Ghats said that would please you, he said that you would be more likely to like a girl that was half English. Minister Ghats said you would find anything else you needed in there," she nodded towards the wardrobe. She put her hand to the top button of her dress and undid it slowly and said, "is there anything else you want?"

I laid the suit on the bed and took her by the arm and led her to the door and said, "thank Minister Ghats for his hospitality and tell him I'm not old enough for young girls', so for the time being I'll stick to women." I closed the door and locked it, there was a knock on the door and she said, "Mr Green, Mr Green she whispered, my name is Elizabeth." I went back into the bathroom. I was surprised at Minister Ghats, and myself. I got into the bath, it was cool. I bathed and lay on the bed thinking about all that had happened to me over the last few days, and drifted off into a light sleep.

The dinner suit fitted well, I felt good and I was hungry, I closed the lounge door, locked it and put the key in my pocket. I walked down the hall and stairs, Jennah Ghats waved to me from the far side of the club lounge and I made my way through the chairs to him. His four friends were still with him, they were all wearing evening dress, they stood up and looked as if they wanted to shake hands again, so I said "good evening, gentlemen" and sat down. They all sat down and Ghats said, "shall we go into dinner, Mr Green? or would you like an aperitif?"

I said "I'd rather eat," so we all stood up and Jennah Ghats led the way to the dining room. It was a long room with three rows of tables down it, a row each side and one down the centre, the ceiling was sprinkled with chandeliers. We sat at a table in the middle of the centre row, it was a large round table. Ghats said I should sit next to him, and left the others to sort themselves out. The President of the Traction Engine Company sat on my other side, he was a fat man and he sweated a lot. A waiter came over and opened a bottle of champagne and filled our glasses, Ghats held the glass of wine and said, "fortunately the English left us a well-stocked cellar," he raised his glass and said "To India," and I said to the "well stocked English cellar", and we drank the wine it was great to have chilled champagne. for a change. Some more waiters served the first course, a small curry dish that was very hot, and poured more champagne. Ghats said he had been to England many times and liked it, and had fond memories of boating on the Thames, and afternoon tea on the lawns of the French Horn at Sonning, I said that's nice and wondered if I'd got mixed up with the wrong people by mistake, or maybe everyone else was wrong, and the Mughal was an Anglo Indian Friendship Society. There was more small talk with each one in turn saying how they had liked Stratford-on-Avon, or Westminster Abbey, and we were all jolly good pals, but I couln'nt help feeling there was an undercurrent of tension.

When the meal was finished the waiters cleared the table and brought coffee cups and brandy glasses and stood a decanter of brandy in the centre of the table. A waiter filled the cups and left the silver coffee pot next to the decanter. As Ghats poured the brandies he said, "now then, Mr Green, what do you think of the boy, The Messiah?"

I sipped my coffee and said, "I don't know," I didn't want to go one way or the other in case it was the wrong way.

Ghats snapped his fingers and a waiter brought a box of Havana cigars and left them on the table. Ghats took a gold cigar cutter from his pocket, snipped the end of one and handed it to me, saying, "good, good." The others each had a cigar but had to do their own snipping, a waiter struck a match and lit my cigar. "Mr Green, you have been in India long enough to know that the great sickness of the country is poverty, the poverty is here because there is not advancement, the Country stands still in spite of the hundred years' effort by your Country, yes you gave us a train system to be envied, and local government, but there is still great poverty, it stands still for one reason, Mr Green, religion, or I should say religions. There are over five hundred million people in India, about two hundred million are Hindus, and Sikhs the other two hundred million are made up from many different religions; there are even about six million Christians. The Hindus evolved the cast system and they can never be united,, the other religions are close knit communities, all separated from each other. So you see as India is today there is no hope of uniting the country. But," he puffed at his cigar and blew the smoke towards the ceiling, "but now we have the Messiah, and with him the hope of uniting India for the first time in its history."

I said, "how do you do you think that will come about?"

"Well, we can guarantee Government recognition of the boy for a start. We control the newspapers, and through our benevolent acts in the past we hold a certain amount of sway in the academic institutions that matter. In short, Mr Green, we are going to sponsor the boy.

"Of course we don't intend to interfere with him in any way, he will do what he has to do. But we will help him, we spread the word, and through him we will unite India." He took a sip of brandy and leaned back in his chair and puffed on his cigar; he looked pleased, they all looked pleased.

I filled my glass from the decanter and my cup from the pot and said, "I don't want to appear dense, Mr Ghats, but it all seems cut and dried, what do you want with me?"

He smiled, "international recognition, Mr Green, you are a respected member of a respected newspaper, with you launching the story in London at the same time as we break the news over here the world will recognise the new Messiah we will convince everyone. That the boy will unite the country It is very important that at the same time as we gain independence, A united India will become united by a new religion as India becomes a country with one religion united behind the Messiah, with a united people nothing can stop the advancement of our country, we will take our place among the major countries of the world. As he had been speaking he grown more agitated, leaning forward in his chair., and gesticulating, he sat back now, and glanced around the table at the group, When World News releases the story it will soon be taken up by the leading newspapers of every other country in the World. There will be a mass pilgrimage to India, millions of people bringing millions of pounds, and dollars, and gold. In a matter of ten years we could provide homes and schools and a decent standard of living." He seemed finished and sat back in his chair.

I said, "there's just one problem, Mr Ghats, what if the boy isn't the Son of God?"

"That is no problem, Mr Green, as long as people think he is that is all that matters."

I said, "what about the million who come carrying their pounds and dollars, it may matter to them."

"Mr Green, last night on the streets of Delhi three English soldiers died, it is a long way to the Airport for a lone English man, but we don't want to think of those unpleasant things do we? To show how grateful we are that you honoured us with your presence this evening, we have a little gift for you." He took a small Chamois leather pouch from his pocket and opened it, and emptied it. Out of the bag ran six large deep red rubies, they looked like a patches of blood on the white tablecloth I hoped they weren't portentous. I picked them up, and rolled them in my hand, they were cold, and felt expensive.

"Just a small gift, Mr Green for your help."

They look like an expensive gift ?they could buy a lot of help,. How much ?

"About ten thousand pounds." I dropped them into the leather pouch one at a time. It wasn't as if they had changed my mind. I was going to send the story anyway, I had been convinced the boy was genuine as far as I was concerned the boy was the what he seemed and anyway if I didn't send the story someone else would. I poured myself a large brandy and drank it, then put the leather pouch in my pocket and said, "When do you want the story sent, Mr Ghats?"

He smiled, they all smiled, Ghats called for champagne, "in about a week, Mr Green, you must send a despatch tomorrow and say that you think the boy is genuine and that you will send the full story in a week, we will be ready then." The waiter brought the champagne and we all toasted India. It was early the next morning when we all shook hands. I was drunk by then, but I managed to keep a straight line across the dining room and through the lounge, I did an unintentional Fred Astair routine on the stairs, then steadied myself, danced around a bit more on the stairs, but made it to my door in one piece. I unlocked it and went in, I didn't put the light on but went straight to the bedroom and undressed and left my clothes on the floor. I pulled back the covers and fell into the bed, my hand touched something warm and soft and a little voice said, "it's Elizabeth, Mr Green, please don't throw me out, Mr Ghats will be very angry with me if I don't please you."

I lay back on the bed, my head was spinning, I took hold of her warm little hand and said, "then you'd better please me, hadn't you?"

I opened my eyes and I was awake, it was morning and my head was pounding. Elizabeth stood at the bottom of the bed getting dressed, she looked more like a school girl than ever

. What do you say to a school girl the morning after, "thank you very much, Miss, I'll give you full marks for that"? I know that child marriages are all the rage in India, but that didn't help my conscience any, so I closed my eyes. When she had gone I got out of bed and felt through the dinner suit for the rubies to make sure that hadn't been a dream. I found the leather pouch and tipped the rubies into my hand. I had to take Minister Ghats word that they were rubies. I remember reading somewhere that real gem stones were always cold. They felt cold and they sparkled, and they looked very expensive.

I got dressed and went downstairs nursing a sore head to the dining room and had breakfast, then walked through to the entrance hall and asked the porter for Minister Ghats. He looked at me as if I was something that had been washed up on the beach. It was a relaxed sort of curiosity, he smiled and put his hands in the air like an Italian, and said, "I'm sorry," then carried on with his work.

I asked him where the main post office was, this time he could help, he even said he was pleased to, and called me, sir. "Go to the bottom of Chandi Chauk and turn left, it was a big building, I couldn't miss it .but take care Mr Green, Lord Mountbatten arrived yesterday, and there are many peoples in town all hoping to see him.

I left the club and turned left and started to edge my way through the crowds in the direction he had told me, and there was Achmed walking beside me, he smiled and I smiled, I was glad to see him. We found the post office, a great Victorian monster with ceilings a hundred feet high. I sent the telegram:

"Looks like the real thing stop Could be bigger than World War three, stop Full story in a few days stop Arthur."

I didn't feel guilty, it was what I thought, and anyway Ghats and his friends probably used rubies like that for their cuff-links. I asked Achmed if he wanted to go back to Ranpure right away, he said it would be best to go very early the next morning and do the journey in one day.

I said, "that was fine by me and that we could spend the rest of the day looking around Delhi." And then I remembered the band I was supposed to book for the Rain Feast, and didn't have Jahmel's list. We spent the next few hours walking around looking for a band. Achmed asked his relations and friends but we got nowhere. Late in the afternoon I found some soldiers and asked them if there was a service man's club nearby; there were three of them, two Englishmen and a Scot. They were pleased and excited to meet someone from home, they said they would take me to the club, but only if I went as their guest. I looked around for Achmed, but he had gone, he knew he wouldn't be welcome at a British Service Man's Club. I looked around again into the crowd, I knew he wouldn't be far away, but I couldn't see him.

The soldiers introduced themselves on the way, Jock was from Glasgow, the Gorbals and looked as hard as iron, he said thumping the wogs gave him a lot of pleasure. Joe was from Clapton, near where I was born in the East End, he said they didn't worry him and he only thumped people if they looked they were going to thump him, he had a pencil moustache and looked like George Raft. If he was stationed at home he looked the type to organise coach trips from the camp, and get forty people into a thirty seater coach, but he'd probably have something organised wherever he was. The other one was Robert, he spoke very well, and kept his opinions to himself, but they all seemed to get on pretty well. The army is a great leveller. The Club was called the Union Jack Club, there was a tattered Union Jack hanging limply over the entrance. As we went in Jock started to tell us how he'd caught two wogs taking it down one night and how he'd given them a good hiding.

Inside was like a home from home, like a typical public Bar, through a curtain beside the Bar I could see someone bending over a snooker table, there was a game of darts going on in the corner. As we passed by the board one of the players shouted Private McGregor what

the bloody hell do you think you're playing at? you know there are no
civilians allowed in here without an officer. He was big and he was
a sergeant and he started across the room towards us. I stepped into
his path, I'm sorry, sergeant, I didn't realise I would get the lads into
trouble, but I'm a reporter on the World News and I've been sent over
here to report on the conditions of the British soldier in India. I waved
my press card at him, and said I'd better leave.

He took the card and looked at it and shouted loud enough to
make sure he had an audience. "A reporter, eh? sent to India, eh? want
to know about the lot of the British soldier eh?" Everyone had stopped
talking and was looking at us. He handed me the card and put his
face close to mine, I could see the veins standing out at the side of his
head. "Well, I'll tell you, Mr Arthur bloody Green, it's a bastard, a
bastard, don't stand there like a spare one, McGregor, get Mr Green a
pint." He smiled and let the audience go, the snooker balls cracked into
each other and the darts thudded into the board, everyone relaxed.
He guided me to the bar and took the pint from Jock McGregor and
handed it to me and said, "get that down you, Arthur, it's the only
decent beer in Delhi, so enjoy it while you can."

As I took the pint he said, "my name is Sergeant Michael Jones,
Mick to my friends and I live at 47, Wellington Avenue, Leeds, just in
case you want to mention it in the article," and he winked.

I put the pint on the bar and pretended to write it in my notebook.
He looked pleased and said, "now drink up, Arthur, bet you haven't
tasted beer like that since you left Blighty." He ordered two more pints
and then looked around. Jock, Joe and Robert were standing behind
him and he said, "I suppose you lot want a drink too," he shouted over
my shoulder, "make that five pints," and said "how we won the war
with soldiers like that I'll never know, that's off the record, of course,
just my manner of speaking, they're not a bad bunch really."

When we had our pints, he said, "now, Arthur, how can we help
you? you ask the questions and we'll supply the answers, won't we
lads?"

Joe gave the V sign at the back of his head and mouthed some
obscenity, and the other two nodded ande said, "yes Sarge."

I took out my notebook again and asked them questions about the
food, their living conditions, how they got on with the Indians, and

pretended to take notes. When we had finished I took the Sergeant on one side and asked him if he could help me with a personal problem. I told him that while I was in India I had been told to get a story on a man called Jahmel who had a Hotel at Ranpure, and that he was sympathetic towards the British. I told him that I had just come back from Ranpure and that the man Jahmel, had arranged a reception on Saturday for a Brigadier General Smythe, and he had asked me to organise a band while I was in Delhi."

He said, "how far is this Ranpure?"

I said, "just a few hours up the road." He thought for a minute and said, "well there are a few lads in the division who make up a band of sorts," but he didn't think the C.O. would agree.

I said, it was a pity and that the Brigadier General would obviously be very grateful to whoever provided the music, especially if it was a military band.

He thought about it again and said, "well, I suppose I could organise some forty-eight hour passes," and if he went along himself to see they didn't get into trouble, he thought it might be arranged.

I said, "Sergeant, that's wonderful, I'll see to it personally that the Brigadier General knows that they sacrificed their weekend leave to provide him with music."

We went back to the bar and I wrote the name and address of the Imperial down and the directions how to get there, and gave it to him. We started drinking again and the Sergeant told us a joke about a man who went into hospital to have a bad leg amputated. After the operation the man woke up the next morning and the doctor came to his bedside and said, "I've got two things to tell you, my man, one is very good and one is very bad."

So the man said, "well you'd better tell me the bad news first,"

So the doctor said, "I'm afraid we've taken off the wrong leg, so he said, my God doctor, that's terrible, what's the good news, "the Sergeant started to explode with laughter, he caught his breath and said, "the other leg is getting better." He let himself go now and bent double with laughter, gasping for air, the three soldiers had heard it before and looked at as the other soldiers looked on, they obviously heard it before.

Just then the door burst open and a soldier ran into the room screaming, "Sergeant, sergeant, they've got Nipper and Jonesy down by the gas works, they're beating hell out of them." Everyone dived for the door, tables were overturned and glasses crashed to the floor. The Sergeant grabbed hold of me and said, "come on, Green, if you want to see how we get on with the natives stay with me," and we followed the others out into the road. It was dark outside. About twenty of us had run out of the Club and we soon got strung out as we ran down the winding lanes and alley's, the Sergeant soon forced his way to the front and like a good news hungry reporter I stayed with him. The sound of the heavy army boots clicked and echoed around the low slum lanes, we turned a corner and there was the gas works, surrounded by a high wire fence. The two soldiers lay in front of an iron gate, they were both unconscious and bleeding, and alone. The Sergeant shouted, "Jock you go that way," the Scot and half the men followed the wire fence in one direction, the rest of us followed Sergeant Jones the other way, nobody seemed very interested in the injured men. We met Jock and the other men on the far side, nobody had seen anything, we stood there puffing and looking around into the darkness. Suddenly someone shouted 'there' and raced across the road, past some spindly trees and into the shadows of the houses, we followed close behind. We caught sight of some shadowy figures disappearing down a narrow lane, we raced to the lane and looked down it. Six Indians stood half-way down the narrow alley pushing each other, they seemed lost, unable to make up their minds what to do. We looked past them and saw why, Jock McGregor stood at the far end of the alley, his belt was in his hand, the buckle end hanging free. As we watched a couple of other soldiers ran up behind him and took off their belts and started to walk slowly down the alley. The Sergeant and some of the others took off their belts and we closed in on the Indians, one of them started to hammer on a door, he was shouting and crying. Jock McGregor was first into them, the belt whining through the air and thudding into the bodies. The others joined in, the Indians tried to break their way through, but were punched back, the coarse flowing robes were pulled from them until they were naked. The heavy brass buckles bit into their bodies, they tried vainly to fend off the blows until they sank one by one into a bloody pile. Sergeant Jones wiped his belt buckle with his handkerchief and threw it away, saying "right lads let's see how Nipper and Jonsey' are."

The soldiers on the far side kicked their way through the bodies and we all walked up the alley. I felt sick, I tasted the vomit in the back of my throat and swallowed to try to keep it down.

The two soldiers still lay at the foot of the gates. We picked up the bodies and started back towards the Union Jack Club, one of the men had run on ahead to get a doctor and some stretchers.

I said to the Sergeant, "I'd better leave you now, Sarge', my billets in the other direction." I stepped back into the shadows, I didn't want him to see me shaking. He grabbed my hand and shook it, saying, "right lad, got a bit of local colour eh? Now mind how you go, it's not like London here you know, or maybe it is eh? Don't forget, lad, Sergeant Michael Jones, 47 Wellington Avenue, Leeds." He marched off into the darkness.

I leant back against a wall, "Arthur," it was the sergeant, "Arthur," I said "yes."

"See you Saturday."

I said "yes," and was sick.

I straightened up and wiped my mouth and eyes with my handkerchief, then I caught sight of something moving in the shadows, I started to run, I stumbled in the darkness and felt someone grab my arm. I kept running and tried to shake off the hand, and a voice said, "that's a fine way for a blood brother to act". It was Achmed, I looked at him, I tried to see if he knew what had happened, but I couldn't tell, and I didn't want to talk about it.

He said, "it's a bit late to get fixed up with somewhere to stay, we had better make a start for Ranpure."

I agreed and he led the way through the back streets to the car. I sank into the front seat, it was, comforting and safe. We found our way through the dark sleeping city and onto the open road. I wound my window down, the air was cold and clear. We drove through the night, the car headlights picking out a thousand pairs of inquisitive eyes, and I fell asleep.

I awoke as thin pencils of light told us that the sun was coming. While the great yellow disc struggled to free itself from a distant hill we stopped at a village and Achmed went to a door and knocked.

A moment later it was opened and a woman stepped out into the morning light and hugged Achmed. He waved at me to come over and we all went into the low house. Achmed said that she was a relative, and that she had told him to tell me that I was very welcome. She made us hot tea and chapattis on an open fire and I felt warm for the first time since last night.

We left the house and drove on, the roads were getting busier now, the great overladen lorries bounced crab like along the road, almost toppling over, and the Ox carts creaked their way on never ending journeys. The farm workers were in the fields and the flies started to dance in the sunlight. We left the tarmac road and bumped our way through the back streets of Ranpure, till we came to the Imperial. The market traders were sitting beside their fruit and vegetable stalls, and the beggar boy sat in the corner watching us.

I reached over and got my bag from the back seat, and said, "about last night, Achmed."

He put up his hand and stopped me speaking, saying, "there are good men and there are bad men always and everywhere, and last night is a long time ago."

I got out and watched the car as it left the square, then walked into the Hotel and up to my room. I threw my bag down and pulled back the mosquito net around the bed and started to undress. I emptied my pockets onto the side table, I'd forgotten the rubies, I picked up the leather pouch and undid it and emptied the rubies into my hand. I wondered how many men had died taking them from the ground, died for nothing, they'd probably finish up in the ground again when everything else was gone. I put them back in the pouch and put it under the pillow, got into bed and went to sleep.

My watch was still not going, but the lack of sound from the square told me it must be near midday. I bathed and washed the dust of Delhi from my body and wished I could wash my mind, wipe away the memory of last night, but I couldn't, it would be there for ever. Its brightness would fade, but it would be there for ever. I would stand in a thousand pub bars and listen, then tell my story about the darkness in the slum streets of Delhi, it was part of me.

Downstairs in the hall, Rhani was talking to a dozen women and boys. When she saw me she ran to the foot of the stairs and said,

"Arthur, thank God you are all right. When did you get back? I was so worried." Then she said something to the people behind her and they left. She took my arm as I reached the foot of the stairs and said, "what happened? did you see Jennah Ghats?"

"Yes, I saw him. I stayed the night at the Colonial Club."

"Well, what did he say?"

"He said they are going to sponsor the boy, they're going to make sure the right people know of him as soon as possible. They just want me to send my story at the right time, that's all."

"What did you say?"

"I said, I would."

"When is the right time?"

"In about a week."

"Good," she looked pleased, "now we must get you some food, you must be hungry." We walked through to the dining room and she rang a bell, a houseboy came in and she said something to him and he left, then we sat at the table and waited.

Rhani said, "I'm glad you came back early, there is so much to do, we would be glad of your help. The Rain Feast only a week and a half away and the decorations haven't been started yet."

I said, "I'll do what I can, but when it is cooler I am going to the plantation, it is important that I see the man who was brought back from the dead."

"All right," she said, "but when you return you must promise to help." She smiled and looked relaxed and happy. The houseboy came in carrying a plate of steaming curry and some coarse bread. As I started to eat, she said, "It's been like old times here, we've been taking on staff and sending messengers with invitations, planning the food. Jahmel has been meeting the townspeople to arrange a procession, he's even been trying to get some fireworks, I haven't seen him so happy for years. I hope it all goes well for his sake."

When I had finished eating, she said, "I think we will make it your special job to decorate the ball-room, come along I'll show you." She stood up and we left the dining room and went along a corridor, half way down the hall on either side were the kitchens. I looked in as we passed, some of the women I had seen in the hall were talking to Charley. Rhani opened the door at the end of the hall and we walked into the ball-room, it was lower than the rest of the Hotel and we went down three steps to the floor. It ran across the back of the Hotel and was about thirty feet wide. It smelt dusty, the far wall was covered with the same red velvet curtains that hung at the windows of the main Hotel building. I walked across and drew them back one by one, they were hung on brass rods and as I tugged them back great clouds of dust puffed from them, behind them were French windows that opened out into a small walled garden that was covered in weeds and long grass. When the curtains were drawn I walked back opening the windows, and as a breeze found its way in, it stirred up the dust from the floor and curtains sending the motes dancing into the air like tiny snowflakes, as it filled the air. Rhani ran through into the garden holding her sari to her mouth.

I held a handkerchief to my mouth and looked around. It was not in keeping with the rest of the Hotel, it had none of the Victorian trappings. The walls were plain plaster and set with oil lamps. There was a stage at one end about two feet high, with some music stands with faded sheet music on them, and an old Grand piano, there was an eerie forgotten sad feel to the room Around the edge of the floor against the walls were chairs thick with dust, it looked odd and out of keeping and didn't do the Imperial justice. I walked across the floor beneath the great faceted dome that Jahmel had mentioned and out into the garden.

Rhani stood in the long grass, she looked as if she was going to cry, "Oh, Arthur, it's terrible, we haven't been in there for years, I didn't think it would as bad as that.

I said, "it's not that bad, at least the curtains didn't fall down. You'll just have to get everybody you can spare and get it washed and cleaned, you'll have to get it organised right away, it'll be all right." I put my arm around her, it was good to touch her again, to feel her close to me, "everything will be all right, you'll see."

She looked up at me, "do you think so, Arthur, do you really think so?"

"yes, but you will have to start right away."

She seemed to cheer up a bit and said, "well, we can certainly try."

She left me and went back through the ball-room. I followed a few minutes later and she was in the kitchen talking to Charley.

I called to her from the door, "Rhani, I'm going to the plantation soon, what is the man's name, the man who Frank brought back to life.

She looked at me and said, "Sufti Nareems, he will be near Frank. Go to the stable they will give you a horse."

I left the Imperial and walked across the square and down the lane towards the stable, the needlewomen were coming out of their houses and resuming their work under the shades.as I got further from the town old men appeared from the shade, walking towards the fields. Now that the sun had passed its peak the country was coming alive again.

The plantation road was packed with pilgrims, they were silent and looked tired but happy, I pushed through them and crossed the monsoon ditch and followed the path to the stable. The boy had seen me coming and had a horse saddled when I got there. He held it while I mounted and I trotted around the edge of the field and joined the plantation road. I edged my way through the crowd onto the road and set off at a slow trot down the middle, the crowds parted as they heard the horse and I made good time, there were more pilgrims than ever, families sitting in the shade of trees, cooking and resting,

The clearing in front of the bungalow was packed and I had to dismount and lead the horse around the crowds. I tied the horse at the back of the bungalow and walked round to the front, up on to the veranda and knocked at the door. Mrs Wilson opened the door, she was carrying a case of powdered milk in one arm, a sheet trailed over the other. She looked surprised, "Mr Green, just the man I need, come in." She handed me the sheet, "here tear this into strips."

I took the sheet and went inside. There were cardboard boxes piled up in the centre of the room, some with powdered milk stencilled on the side, others with dried egg and others with rice.

Mrs Green was bustling from room to room, she had already torn up one sheet and the strips were laying over one of the boxes. I started to tear up my sheet into strips and laid them with the others.

When she bustled through the next time I said, "is Sufti Nareem here? I'd like to see him."

She stopped and looked at me, "Sufti? No, he's gone, they've all gone, Frank, Mr Wilson, Sufti, Majid, they've all gone. I'm the only one here now, Mr Green, will you please get on with the bandages."

She disappeared into Frank's room, I ran after her tearing strips off the sheet as I went. "What do you mean Mrs Wilson, gone, where have they gone?"

She pulled the sheets off the bed and pushed them into my arms and said, "tear these into bandages, and please hurry, they'll be here in a minute and I must be ready."

I followed her into the lounge tearing the sheets, "Mrs Wilson will you please tell me where they've gone," she was standing on a chair taking the curtains down, she said over her shoulder.

They've gone to the plains of Lucknow, there's a Cholera epidemic sweeping through the area, a Red Cross Field Hospital Unit came through here two days ago, they went with them. They had to leave these here," she pointed at the boxes, "to make room for them, there's another Hospital Unit due here at any time to pick them up, I'm going with it. I've been tending to the pilgrims since they left, but there's not enough water, some of them are dying, but they won't leave until they've seen Frank."

She got down and put the curtains on the boxes then started to take the others down. She threw one to me and said, "put that with the others, they may keep some poor mite warm, and please hurry with those bandages."

I'd just finished tearing up the last sheet when we heard a car horn in the distance. Mrs Wilson opened the front door and we watched a large canvas topped lorry with a red cross painted crudely on the side, edge its way up the Lower Road. It was covered with laughing Indian children hanging on the sides, on the roof and mudguards. It came across the clearing scattering the crowds and stopped in front of the bungalow, the children jumped down and ran off laughing and shouting. The driver got down slowly, he looked about thirty, but had grey hair and wore glasses, his eyes were red rimmed with tiredness .Through the open door of the lorry I could see a woman asleep in the passenger seat. The driver came up the steps of the bungalow and said, "I'm Doctor Scott, I believe there are some provisions to pick up." He held out his hand limply, he was about five feet eight and stocky, his face was heavily lined and there were dark patches beneath his eyes, his grey hair was long and uncombed and grew down over his collar.

As I took his hand he closed his eyes and swayed and gripped my hand hard to steady himself. He opened his eyes again and I said, "I'm Arthur Green, and this is Mrs Wilson, you'd better come in and have a rest while I load the lorry."

He straightened himself and said, "thank you but, there's no time to rest."

Mrs Wilson said she would make a cup of tea and we started carrying the boxes outside. When we loaded the lorry we sat on the veranda for a few moments, and drank the tea. The children were laughing and climbing all over the lorry again.

Doctor Scott put down his empty cup and stood up, he pulled himself to his feet by holding onto the veranda rail, he swayed again and held onto the rail. "Thank you for the tea Madam, but we must be on our way again," he started to walk unsteadily down the steps.

Mrs Wilson ran down the steps beside him, "shall I ride in the front or the back, Doctor?"

He stopped and looked at her, "you will not ride in the front or the back, Madam, you are not coming with us."

Mrs Wilson looked stunned, "but, Doctor you don't understand my husband is there with Frank and Majid and Sufti, my family, I must be with them."

The Doctor turned and looked at her and said, "Madam if Doctor Peabody sees fit to leave much needed provisions behind and fill his vehicle with a bunch of bloody amateurs that's up to him, but I do not intend to do the same." He turned and walked towards the lorry.

Mrs Wilson ran after him and grabbed his arm, "Doctor, you don't understand, I have to go, my husband is there with the new Messiah the son of god."

He pulled his arm free and climbed slowly into the cab. She was crying now, "please, Doctor, please you've got plenty of room," she was sobbing uncontrollably. I ran down the steps and put my arm around her.

He looked down at us and said, "I'm sorry but we need trained medical personnel, there are enough amateurs up there already getting in our way, anyway if your Frank is the Son of God his Father will get you up there a lot quicker than I can won't he?"

Mrs Wilson turned to me and put her arms around my neck like a child, she had given up now, and the tears ran down her cheeks and her body jerked with sobbing.

I pushed her aside and stepped up onto the running board and said, look Doctor I am sure we can be of help, Mrs Wilson is a trained nurse, I lied but it was no use, the Doctor wound up the window, and I heard the sound of the crunching gears as he tried to drive away.

Mrs Wilson clung onto me as and I helped her up the steps into the veranda she sank onto a packing case as we watched the lorry bump erratically through the pilgrims towards the lane.

As the lorry approached the Lane the horn sounded, and it went on and on and on, something was wrong, we ran across the open ground towards the vehicle, I could see the Doctor slumped against the steering wheel and yanked open the door he slid slowly sideways into my arms, the woman in the passenger seat was awake now and together we pulled him off the wheel. She said, "is this the Wilson bungalow?"

I said, "yes," she looked angry, "he's a fool, I did not think we would get even this far." She was German and spoke the precise English that the Germans use. "He must rest; he has been driving for twenty-four hours.

"She had on khaki British Army trousers and shirt with red cross arm bands around each arm. She took his wrist and looked at a large wrist watch, then she looked at me and said, "Mr?" I said "Green,"

"Mr Green, I am telling you this man is very tired and weak, he needs rest and much of it."

I said "do you know the way to the Lucknow plains, the Cholera site.?

She thought for a minute and said "yes, I think so."

"Good then I'll drive and the Doctor can sleep in the back." I jumped down and ran around to the back of the lorry, she came around the other way and said, "Did he say you could come? he was not very happy about non-medical people getting in the way

"Of course, he said we could come, we were just getting our things together when he collapsed."

She looked doubtful. I said, "what's your name?" "Nurse Mullan."

"Right, Nurse Mullan, if you could clear some of the boxes in the back, we can lay him on the floor." I helped her into the back of the lorry and ran back into the bungalow.

Mrs Wilson was standing on the veranda looking anxiously at us"Come on Gladys, we're going to Lucknow. "what do you mean? what's happened ?"

"Well I think old Dracula has missed his daily pint of blood or something, anyway he's passed out, and I told the Nurse that he said we could go. I don't think she believed me, but that doesn't matter, does it?"

She got to her feet, "but you weren't going, I don't know when we will get back."

I handed her a coat and said, "well, I've got to see Sufti and it looks like I may not get another chance, so it had better be now."

We walked out to the lorry and I introduced her to Nurse Mullan. We carried the Doctor to the back and laid him on the floor. Mrs Wilson put some of the curtains under his head. I ran to the back of the bungalow and untied the horse and slapped its rump, it trotted off towards the Burning Hill and across country towards the stables, then we all got into the cab. I started the engine and drove across the clearing through the crowds, the boys were climbing all over the lorry again. I drove down the Lower Road and stopped at the Junction with the plantation road, the boys jumped off and ran back up the Lower Road shouting and laughing. I looked across at the Nurse, "which way Nurse Mullan?"

We had been driving for about eight hours along Tarmac strip and unmade roads, the, light was fading and there was the constant danger of running off the unmade roads, Nurse Mullan was giving me direction from a torn map by torch light that she held together on the top of a medical folder. I looked into the rear view mirror and saw Doctor Scott looking at me, he didn't look angry, his tired eyes looked at me from the mirror, when I looked again he was gone. Shortly after that we stopped to fill the petrol tank from cans that were in the back of the lorry, before setting off again I looked in the back, the Doctor was still asleep. When dawn broke we were already on the plains of Lucknow, the flat sun baked land seemed to stretch as far as the sun, broken only by clusters of trees.. It was at the edge of one of the larger groups of trees,where the trees were still thin that we saw the other Red Cross Unit, it was parked in a sprawling village that was between the trees, beside the lorry was an army jeep. I stopped beside the other vehicles and we all got out. Mrs Wilson had slept some of the way, but Nurse Mullan had guided me from the Wilson's bungalow for about sixteen hours, after a few hours of staring into the darkness barely lit by the weak lorry headlights the nurse had produced some pills to help us stay awake she said, and I didn't feel too bad, very stiff, but not too tired. She looked terrible, pale, sick, and she got out of the cab like an old woman, I knew I'd feel the same when the effect of the pills had worn off.

We walked around to the back of the lorry, Doctor Scott had already got down, he took Nurse Mullan's arm and they went off into the trees without comment.. Mrs Wilson and I started to unload the provisions. We had just unloaded the last box when a man in a white coat walked out of the trees towards us and introduced himself. "Good morning, I'm Doctor Peabody." We shook hands and I introduced Mrs Wilson. Doctor Peabody asked us if we had been vaccinated against Cholera. I said "I hadn't," Mrs Wilson said that she had, and that she had nursing experience. Doctor Peabody was about sixty, he was roughly six feet tall and very thin, with a black drooping moustache and was very tanned. He said, "Mr Green, I have to thank you for bringing the provisions, Doctor Scott told me that he passed out and that you were obliged to drive the lorry up here, and we are all very grateful, but I'm afraid you'll have to leave, to put it bluntly, Mr Green you'll not be of much use to us, and it's senseless that you risk getting Cholera just to stand about watching us work, sadly we are out of insulin. Come along we'll see that you get some food before you leave"

We all started to walk into the trees, he smiled at me, "don't worry, Mr Green you won't have to walk; Captain Jameson of our mobile unit is here and he will be leaving for Delhi in an hour or two, to get some more insulin, you can go with him.

As we walked into the trees it got darker and the ground grew muddy. There were several fires burning and the smoke hung in the air, there were people and bodies everywhere, lying beneath the trees, huddled around the fires or just standing about. They all watched us as we walked through, Mrs Wilson was carrying her box of bandages and curtains.

Doctor Peabody waved his arms around, "everything is wrong, we couldn't be in a worse place, the forest is over an underground stream or something, it's full of stagnant water, the water carries the Cholera, we try to teach them to boil the water, but they won't learn. With Cholera the body gets dehydrated, constant vomiting and diarrhoea dehydrates the body. They drink the water and if it isn't boiled they re-infect themselves, it's a vicious circle. Even with the insulin there's little hope, unless they boil the water, it's a question of education more than medicine at this stage. They come in here to get away from the sun, we couldn't be in a worse position .the monsoons due at any time and then the whole of the Lucknow Plains will be under water, we've got to get them to higher ground somehow. There are thousands of them around the edges of this forest, and we've got no transport and most of them are too sick to move, I'm afraid it's hopeless, it's all a matter of education." He seemed to be talking to himself now, breaking off to tend a vomiting child or take the pulse of a woman or man lying on the muddy ground, "a matter of education. They won't even help themselves because of the caste system they won't even talk to each other, education is what is needed as well as medicine. We've got a hospital tent set up, the worst ones are there. I don't know what we will do when the rains come, it's hopeless he kept mumbling to himself"

We walked on through the bodies, the smoky air was filled with the smell of vomit and excretia, and rotting flesh, the bodies were getting thicker, sometimes lying across the path and we had to step over them.

Doctor Peabody was talking to himself all the time as if he was trying to distract himself from what was around us. It was getting darker, and with the vomiting bodies all around us and the smoky stinking air, it was like walking into hell, a half-remembered nightmare. I was glad he wouldn't let me stay. The hospital tent was about fifty feet long and low, it was set up in a small clearing, but the trees touched over it, and it was dark, though not as dark as the rest of the forest. There were bodies in rows all around the tent, some on low camp beds others lying on the ground. There were half a dozen Doctors and Nurses bending over them. Doctor Peabody gave Mrs

Wilson and I a surgical mask, we put them on and went into the low tent. There were bodies lying close together on camp beds down each side of a centre gangway on wooden slats. More Doctors and Nurses, including Doctor Scott and Nurse Mulhan were doing what they could for the patients, the surgical masks kept out some of the smell, but it was still terrible.

We walked slowly down the centre gangway and out of the tent at the other end. There was a smaller tent about a hundred yards away through the trees and Doctor Peabody led us there. It was a Field kitchen, the front flaps were pulled back and we could see two cooks inside preparing food. Outside was a large wooden scrubbed table, a white coated man was sitting at the table, his head cradled in his arms asleep. We sat down and Doctor Peabody went inside, as I sat down I felt tiredness creep through my body slowly like a cloud passing across the sun. Mrs Wilson, still clutched her box of bandages, she looked shocked. She sat there, clutching her box looking around her, her eyes were wide as if she couldn't believe what she saw. Doctor Peabody came out of the kitchen carrying two plates of watery stew, half cooked powdered eggs swam about on the greasy surface. Mrs Wilson took the plates and said, "my husband, doctor, Mr Wilson, have you seen him"

"He's about somewhere. Said the doctor kindly, you'll run into him sooner or later

." He started to walk away and then came back. "Would you come to the hospital tent when you have eaten, we need all the help we can get at the moment." He turned to me and held out his hand, "Thank you again, Mr Green, I may not see you again before you leave, so I'll wish you a safe journey."

I stood up and took his hand in mine, I wanted to tell him how much I admired him, how I envied his strength and humanity, but I said nothing, and he turned and walked towards the big tent and I sank back into my chair. I was too tired to take off the surgical mask and eat, and I closed my eyes, my body felt heavy and strange, my mind was still active but it seemed to be in the wrong body, a giant's body.

I felt something touch my arm, Mrs Wilson was standing beside me. "I'll say goodbye, Mr Green, we may not meet again, get some rest, you look awful, you had a long tiring drive and those pills will be starting to wear off."

My little tired eyes looked up at her out of a heavy giants body, and we formally shook hands as if saying goodbye having been introduced at a luncheon . She picked up the cardboard box and walked towards the hospital tent. I sat there watching her go, and then I saw Frank, he was walking towards the hospital tent carrying a child in his arms, his white robe was splashed with mud and his feet were bare. I pulled myself to my feet and started to run towards him, tried to call out his name, I felt exhausted but tried to rally, my limbs were out of time with each other, jerking like a puppet. I ran through the trees calling, "Frank, Frank." I got near to him and bumped into a tree and put my arms out to steady myself, and slid slowly to the ground. He smiled and walked towards me, reaching out an arm to help me to my feet, he was carrying a child and laid her in my arms, it was a girl and her face and arms were covered with sores. and grime. He helped me to my feet said, "I think you had better come and sit down, Mr Green, you don't look well, he led me gently away from the tree towards the long table outside the Kitchen tent.

"Look after the baby, look after the child he said." I suddenly felt the tiredness leaving me, and the spirit in me growing, filling up my tired body, reaching every corner as if someone was blowing up a balloon inside me. I opened my eyes and Frank was holding my arm, I felt stronger, elated, almost light headed. I said, "look after the child, Frank, I'll be all right now." But he held my arm until we reached the table and I sat down. I felt the tiredness growing in me again, and looked down at the child in my arms at weak un seeing eyes, and the pok marks and the grime on her lifeless face.

Frank sat next to me his arm around my shoulder and I closed my eyes.

It seemed like only moments later when I looked down at the child again, her skin was clear and her eyes sparkled her face was grubby but unmarked She put her fingers into the bowl of soup and sucked it laughing, I looked up and saw Frank disappearing into the trees towards the sick and dying, I closed my eyes.

"Mr Green, Mr Green, it's time to go."

I opened my eyes, a young man in a Captain's uniform was shaking me. "I'm Captain Jameson, if you are coming we have to go now, it's time to go."

The child was gone, I said, "there was a child here with Frank when I fell asleep, a baby girl, did you see her?"

"No, there was nobody here, the camp is full of children, but I haven't seen any around here. If you're ready, Mr Green we'll have to leave now."

I stood up and looked around for Frank, I couldn't see him. I asked the Captain if he had seen Frank and the child, but he didn't hear me" I looked at my watch, it still was'nt going but by the shade creeping through the trees I guessed I had I'd slept for about-an-hour.

Had I dreamt about Frank and the child, or had I seen a miracle, had Frank performed a miracle because he believed he could, or had I seen a real miracle? had the power of belief overcome everything?

The Captain looked round anxiously, "I don't know Frank, but you'll find the Doctors around the hospital tent."

"No, he's not a doctor, he's an Indian boy about sixteen, tall and slim, a fine young man"

"No, I've been making a list of supplies with Doctor Peabody and Dr.Patel, we've been between here and the hospital tent for most of the time you've been asleep, and the only Indians I've seen, boys or girls have been on their backs. We really will have to go now, Mr Green, I've got to get to Delhi and back, and away from this place before the rains come. I don't think anyone will get out of here once the monsoon start, even the cattle are moveing to higher ground." He turned around and started to walk towards the path that led out of the forest. I looked down at the table, the soup plate, there were splashes of soup on the table .

The sleep had done me good and I felt better, we had just reached the path when I heard someone shouting, "Mr Green, safe journey."

I looked around and saw Mr Wilson. I ran over to him and said, "have you seen Frank?"

"Yes, of course I've seen him, not for a bit mind you, but he's around somewhere."

I said, "thank God! I thought I'd been dreaming."

Mr Wilson gave me a funny sort of smile and said, "you probably have been dreaming, Mr Green, the whole place is like a dream, isn't it? or more like a bloody nightmare." He looked terrible, there was a stubbly beard on his chin and he was covered with mud and looked exhausted.

Captain Jameson shouted, "I'm leaving, Mr Green whether you come with me or not. I can't wait any longer," he was disappearing down the path.

I said, "Mr Wilson when you see Frank will you tell him, what!" what could I say, tell him I believe in him., I said a hurried goodbye to Mr Wilson and good luck." I turned and walked down the path past the bodies.

Mr Wilson shouted, "see you soon, I hope." I walked on through the smoke and the stench and out into the fierce sunlight, it was still early morning. I had been there for less than two hours, and it seemed like a lifetime. I breathed in the air, it was clean and sweet and smokeless.

Captain Jameson had turned the jeep around, he pulled up beside me and I got in. He rammed it into gear and stamped hard on the accelerator. The jeep shot forward onto the dusty track and he said, "I'm going to get to Delhi and back again, and out of it as fast as I can, if they think I'm going to get caught in that bloody death trap when the rains come, they've got another think coming." The little jeep hurtled down the bumpy track and I hung on to the top of the windscreen and the back of my seat until my shoulders ached, and I remembered how Frank had smiled at me as he held the sick child, and then how she had laughed when she put her finger in the soup, bright-eyed and healthy. Had it been a dream, was I already asleep? I'd taken Nurse Mullen's pills to stay awake, had they affected me?

When we got onto the main Delhi road it wasn't so bumpy, and I released my grip and settled down in the seat out of the wind. Captain Jameson and I didn't speak again until late that night. We stopped in front of the Imperial, I thanked him and got out. The jeep roared away from me and he shouted something over his shoulder that I didn't understand. I watched it race out of the square, the headlights lighting everything for a second, and it was gone.

I went up the steps and into the Hotel, every lamp was alight in the long hall, it was bright, then I remembered the Rain Feast. I looked at my watch, it was just midnight and the Rain Feast had officially begun. I heard voices coming from the Bar. I walked quietly down the hall and looked through the crack in the open door. Jahmel and Rhani were standing by the bar surrounded by about a dozen people, four of them were Europeans, a Vicar in a dark suit and dog collar, an Army Chaplain and a middl aged couple in civilian dress, the rest were Indians, some in suits, the others in traditional robes. They were all laughing and talking and Charley was serving drinks. I heard the kitchen door close down the hall behind the stairway, I turned and ran up the stairs as quietly as I could. I didn't want to see anyone or talk to anyone, I'd seen and heard as much as my mind could take and I'd had enough. I went along the hall to my room and lit the lamp by the bed, got undressed and climbed onto the bed and pulled the mosquito net down like a shield. I sank down and felt something hard against my back, it was the leather pouch, I'd forgotten about the rubies and the Murghal

I slept badly, dreaming I was back at the Cholera camp on the Lucknow Plains, and I half awoke sweating and choking on the stench, then I would drift back again into the darkness and smoke.

When I awoke Rhani was sitting on the bed watching me. She said, "Arthur, where have you been? you look terrible, we've been so worried. When the horse came back alone we thought you'd had an accident. Some of the boys went out to look for you and when they didn't find you, I didn't know what to think. The bungalow was empty, it looked as if it had been ransacked, and everyone was gone."

She looked clean, fresh and lovely. I stared at her shutting out the ugliness of the last few days.

"Arthur, what's the matter, what happened?"

I said, "I've been to hell and back again, that's the matter. I've seen and smelt the dead and dying and it has frightened me.

She stretched out a cool hand and stroked my cheek, "what happened?

"When I left you on Thursday afternoon I rode out to the plantation to see Sufti Nareem, but he'd gone, he'd left two days earlier with Frank for the Lucknow Plains, they had all gone except

Mrs Wilson. A Red Cross Unit had stopped at the bungalow on the way to a Cholera camp and they'd talked them into letting Frank and the others go with them. Another Hospital Unit was due to call at the bungalow when I arrived, Mrs Wilson and I went with that."

"To the Lucknow Plains?"

"Yes."

"Arthur, you must be mad, that's over two hundred miles each way."

"I know, I know."

"What made you go?"

"Circumstances arose that made it seem inevitable."

"Did you see Sufti?"

"No."

She jumped up from the bed. "You mean you went two hundred miles to see a man, and then you didn't see him?"

"That's right."

She looked annoyed. "Why ever not?"

"Because I only stayed a few of hours."

She stamped her foot and walked quickly to the window and looked out.

I said, "I only stayed an hour or two because the doctor wouldn't let me stay any longer. I hadn't been vaccinated, and they had run out of vaccine. Have you ever been to a Cholera camp?"

"No .but I know about the camps and Cholera.

"Well if you went to one, and someone told you that you had to leave within an hour, you would be damned glad."

"So it was a wasted journey then?"

"No, not exactly."

"Why?"

"Well, I saw something, or I think I saw something."

"What?"

I felt embarrassed. I didn't want to tell anyone about the miracle, if it was a miracle, I wasn't sure myself.

"Arthur, don't make me drag it out of you word by word, what happened?"

"I drove to the camp without a break, there was a nurse with the unit and she gave me some pills to keep me awake."

"Why were you driving?"

"There was a Doctor Scott in charge of the Unit, he collapsed at the bungalow, and it seemed the natural thing for me to take over. Anyway by the time we got there the pills were wearing off and I felt terrible, exhausted. The doctor in charge told me to come right into the camp to get some food. I was to leave almost immediately with a young Captain who was going to Delhi for supplies. I was sitting down resting when I saw Frank, I started to run towards him, but I was so weak I could barely move, I shouted as loudly as I could and he saw me. He was carrying a child, a baby girl, he brought her to where I was, she was covered with vomit, and poc scars, she looked dead. I could see her quite clearly, he laid her in my arms and took hold of my arm and the tiredness seemed to lift out of me. He took me to where I had been sitting, and then went back and lifted op the girl and held her to him he brought her to me and laid her in my arms, Rhani, there was nothing wrong with her, the sores had gone, and she was happy and smiling. Well, I was so tired then that I fell asleep, when I awoke the child was gone and so was Frank. That's what happened, the trouble is I don't really know if it did happen, maybe the pills made me see things, or perhaps I was already asleep."

Rhani walked over and sat on the bed again, "There's one way you can find out."

"How?"

"By asking Frank."

"Yes, if I see him again."

"You'll have to make sure you do see him again, won't you?"

I said nothing.

"You still don't believe do you, doubting Arthur?"

"I do, well ninety-nine per cent of me does, but there's one per cent floating about somewhere that I can't quite nail down."

Rhani looked angry. "Well, you had better make sure Jannah Ghats doesn't find out, it could be a very expensive one per cent." She smiled quickly as if to cover up her anger. "Poor Arthur you've had a bad time," she leaned forward and kissed me lightly, "but never mind today is the Rain Feast, you must forget everything, we will all forget our troubles." She stood up and said, "you must come down to breakfast as soon as possible, some guests have arrived already and I must introduce you."

When she had gone I lay there thinking about what she had said. I knew I would have to see Frank again and nail down that one per cent. There was a knock on the door and Gomel came in. I hadn't seen him since that first day at the Imperial. He went into the bathroom and ran the bath, then left. I took the rubies from the bed and put them at the bottom of my bag in the wardrobe, then bathed and shaved, put on a clean shirt and went downstairs to breakfast and the guests.

The Hotel was busy, there were houseboys in white coats with trays hurrying about. A large vase of flowers stood on the desk near the front door and everything seemed clean and polished. I stood at the bottom of the stairs and prepared myself mentally, then went into the dining room. More tables had been moved in and there were people sitting at all of them, about twenty in all, mostly Indians. The four Europeans I had seen in the bar last night were sitting at our table which was still in the centre of the room.

The room fell silent as I entered, and they all stared at me. I stood in the entrance for a moment and decided that I would scrounge something in the kitchen rather than face polite breakfast chatter. I turned to leave and someone said, "I say you must be Arthur Green," it was the Vicar. He had left the table and was walking towards me. "My name is Johnson, come along I'll introduce you to the others."

There was no way out, I smiled, as much of a smile as I could manage and followed him to the table. I kept smiling while he introduced us. "Now Mr Green this is Mr and Mrs Granger," they looked like Laurel and Hardy, and she was the fat one. She had fair blotchy skin and was wearing a suit. She gripped my hand like a playful gorilla. Her husband had the same sad surprised look that the thin one had, he sat on the other side of the table and was in two minds about shaking hands, in the end he gave me a sort of bow and sat down. "This is Captain East, our Chaplain, he looks after our soldier's souls. I of course am in the same line of work, but I direct my efforts towards civilians. Mr and Mrs Granger are missionaries and they consider any souls are fair game."

Everybody smiled and I sat down. "What brings you to this part of India, Mr Green?" It was the Chaplain who spoke.

"I've been sent out to see how the British soldiers get on with the natives. There's a general feeling that the British will be leaving India soon and I wanted to see the effect it was having, on both sides."

Mrs Granger said, "if you want to check on the moral of the British soldier you are off the beaten track, aren't you? I think you would find more information in Bombay or Calcutta."

"Yes, I suppose so, but the Cities will be full of reporters, I want to get a fresh approach. I've just been to a Cholera camp on the Plains of Lucknow, I couldn't have done that if I'd been in Bombay or Calcutta, could I?"

We kept chatting through breakfast about India and where the British had gone wrong and about what was going on in England when I had left. There was no sign of Rhani or Jahmel. When we had nearly finished I said, "I've heard some rumours about an Indian boy who claims to be the Son of God, have you heard anything about it?"

There was silence, then the Reverend Johnson said, "we are all the Sons of God, Mr Green."

"Yes, I know that, but I mean the real Son of God, like Jesus."

Then Mr Granger said, "If God had decided to send another Son onto the earth, I don't think he would choose to send him as a parentless peasant boy, to an unknown village in India."

I said, "so you do know about him?"

"No, we have heard the rumours, that's all."

I turned to Captain East and said, "what do you think, Chaplain, is it possible?"

"All things are possible, Mr Green, Jesus was born in very humble surroundings, as we all know, and Joseph, of course, was his father in name only. The boy Frank arrived at the plantation with only his mother, and they were penniless, as Jesus's family was, I've even heard a rumour that the boy has healed a man with a withered arm, there are in fact several points of similarity."

I said, "I understood that the boy claims that he was sent to the earth only a year ago."

Mrs Granger said, "but the people at the plantation say that he has lived there all his life."

I looked at them, they obviously knew all about Frank. I wondered what their opinions would be once the Jennah Ghats publicity machine got under way. Then I said, "what do you think the boy would gain by saying these things?"

Mrs Granger said, "religious cults can be very profitable you know, if they can attract a wealthy following."

I wanted to say, you mean like established religious faiths, but these people would be here all day, so I may as well try and get along with them, so I said. "Do you think a sixteen-year-old native boy could be that devious?"

"No," said Mrs Granger, "somebody has put him up to it."

I was getting a little annoyed now and I said, "how exactly, Mrs Granger would you go about putting a sixteen-year-old boy 'up to' healing a man's withered arm?"

There was an awkward silence, then the Reverend said, Mr Green this is India, and all things are possible in India.

"I think what Mrs Granger meant, Mr Green was that the Indians are basically more simple than Europeans, they find it easier to believe. Let us suppose that someone started the rumour about the healing, I am sure it would be believed by a large proportion of natives that heard of it."

I said, "what you really mean is that the average Indian is more stupid than the average European?"

"No, Mr Green, certainly not. I mean that the Indian has not yet acquired European scepticism."

I was about to tell them what this sceptical European saw at the Lucknow Cholera camp and see if it sent these deeply religious people racing out of the Imperial in search of the truth, when I saw Rhani standing in the doorway, she beckoned to me. I made a few polite remarks about enjoying the conversation and seeing them all later and excused myself. I was seething by the time I got to the doorway. I pulled Rhani out into the hall and said, "do you know what those tireless workers for God have heard all about Frank, and they have dismissed the rumours. You would think that they, above all people would make some effort, some effort be damned, they should run all the way till their feet are bleeding to find out the truth, their bloody complacency makes me sick. Something so enormous has happened and they sit at a breakfast table discussing the rumour like the weather forecast for a Test Match."

Rhani said, "Arthur you shouldn't feel so deeply, Jennah Ghats will do in a day what it would take a thousand of them a year to do." "I wasn't talking about doing, I was talking about believing, maybe Charley was right, the superficial West had lost the ability to believe, maybe cars, televisions and advertising and the pressure of life had robbed us of a lot of things, and we hadn't even realised it, maybe we never would."

Rhani said, "cheer up, you at least will go down in history as the first man to recognise the New God, the New Messiah."

I thought, yes, and I've been to church once in ten years, and that was to start the end of my marriage, but that was one thing Frank said, he wanted to do away with" the places of worship."

Rhani said, "please cheer up, Arthur, everything will be all right, you'll see."

I smiled, and Rhani took my hand and said, "I will show you something that will cheer you up," and she led me down the hall behind the stairs, but I wasn't cheered up, there was something tugging at a corner of my mind, like a kitten tugging at a great black tablecloth.

Rhani threw open the ballroom door, it was a transformation, the floor had been washed and polished and the wood looked rich and warm, the walls had been scrubbed and the brass oil lamps were gleaming. The curtains were clean and bright, and coloured streamers ran from the great glitter dome to every corner of the room. I walked around the room and said with a big smile, "how on earth did you manage all of this without me?" Rhani laughed and said, "you mean in spite of you, don't you?"

"Arthur, thank goodness you're safe, Rhani told me what happened, bit of a rotten do, what?" Jahmel was standing in the doorway, he seemed to fill it. He walked across the ballroom to me, "but you are safely back, that's the main thing, isn't it, old chap?"

I usually had the feeling that Jahmel was doing me a favour by speaking to me, but this time he sounded as if he meant it. "It looks like Frank is on the move, doesn't it? but it doesn't matter, I have just heard from the plantation owners, they have accepted my offer, and as soon as the Rain Feast is decently out of the way we will start on the Shrine."

I said, "I don't think that Frank is too interested in Shrines."

Jahmel laughed, "of course he's not, of course he's not, but I am, Rhani is, the Imperial is."

So that was the way it was going to be, with Jesus it had been the doubters, with Frank it was to be the exploiters. I was about to say something when I remembered the rubies, and I kept quiet.

Jahmel said, "I believe you met some of our guests at breakfast, some more will be arriving later this morning, there will be a cocktail party about midday. The processions will be late this evening, and by the way, old chap if I were you I would sort through the fancy dress now, before the others get a chance to, or you will end up with a Fig Leaf." He thought that was very funny, he was still laughing as he left the room.

Rhani said, "he's right you know, we will go up right away and find you something."

We left the ballroom and walked down the long hall. More guests were arriving and a boy was putting some bags in the hall as we went upstairs, The Imperial was bustling again.

The costumes were kept in the attic rooms and we went up a rickety old stairway to get to them There was every kind of costume you could think of there, all hung neatly around the room with sheets over them. There were animal skins, King's and Queen's dresses and uniforms of every rank. I guessed that was where the Major's uniform came from that Jahmel had given me when I arrived. There were outfits for dandy's and beggars, Emperors and slaves, courtesans and peasants. I tried on a crown but it fell down over my ears and Rhani laughed, next I put on a laurel wreath, part of a Roman Emperor's dress, but the Toga was much too long. I was enjoying myself strutting about and making Rhani laugh, then I found it, Napoleon's three cornered hat. I held the cut-away jacket against me, it seemed as if it would fit, and the hat was perfect.

Rhani was very pleased with my choice. As we were leaving I took hold of her hand and turned her to me and said, "what about when it's all finished, Rhani, when the story is released, the Shrine is built and the Imperial is full again, what about us?"

She looked sad and said, "us, is there an us? one night cannot bridge the differences between India and England, or you and I. One day soon you will go home and you will sit in your office in Fleet Street, you will think of the dirt and the disease and the poverty. You will remember the beggar boy and you will be sad. You will put money into the Red Cross Charity box and tell your friends about the girl in Rhanpure . Love can get very thin when it is stretched across 8,000 miles. I will remember you and be glad, but I must give my heart to India, although I have been brought up to look and sound like an English girl, my deepest feelings are for my country." She gave me a sad sorry little smile and left the room. I gathered up my Napoleon uniform and went downstairs to my bedroom and hung them in the wardrobe.

"Arthur, Arthur," I could hear Jahmel calling my name from below, then the door burst open. "Arthur, what about the band? you didn't take my list, did you manage to arrange anything?"

I had forgotten Sergeant Michael Jones and the Army band. I had pushed that right to the back of my mind, I said, "Yes, I think I have got you a band. I met some British soldiers in Delhi who said they would come out here and play, the only thing is, I told them a Brigadier General would be a guest at the party, it was the only way I could think of getting them to come."

Jahmel said, "I'm afraid we don't have a Brigadier General's uniform or we could get someone to impersonate one. We used to do those sort of things at Cambridge, you know, good fun."

"Well I was just going to tell them that the Brigadier had to cry off at the last minute, had to meet Lord Mountbatten, that will impress them, getting them here was the main thing

Jahmel said, "jolly good old chap. I'll leave it to you then."

"Yes, if they come."

"Well, I hope they come, old chap, we will be in a pretty fix if they don't, but we'll cross that bridge when we come to it. Perhaps I ought to find the old Gramophone just in case" He left the room, and shouted, "don't forget the cocktail party, old chap."

I started to think about the story again and how I could convince the readers of World News about Frank. It wouldn't be so difficult now that Jennah Ghats was going to release the story from this end, but it still wouldn't be easy. It was the sort of story that might just backfire, it may be too much, it might become a sick joke!

'Hello Bill, did you read that story about the new God? New God! I hope he does better than the last one. Yes, it's a rotten way to spend Easter isn't it?" I got my note-book from the wardrobe and read through my first draught, it would have to be tidied up a bit, but it wasn't bad. I wrote another few pages on Majid and my trip to the cholera camp, and the miracle I saw. I padded it out a bit with my trip to Delhi. I left out Sergeant Michael Jones and what happened in the back streets of Delhi that night. There was a knock on the door, it was Charley to tell me that most of the guests had arrived now, and would I care to join them in the bar. I put the note-book away quickly dressed and went downstairs.

The bar was packed and people were spilling out into the hall, the houseboys were busy with bottles of champagne. I hoped that Jahmel's idea about crowds flocking to the Shrine were right. There must have been a hundred people or more here already for the Rain Feast, it would finish him financially, he had already bought the Plantation with money he didn't have.

I could see Jahmel in the bar towering over everybody, the centre of attention. I expect he was telling them about Frank. The people here were all the 'right people' from the area, small-time politicians and traders and leaders from the surrounding villages. When they left they would be telling their friends about Frank, word of mouth was still the best way to spread news in a country like India. One of the houseboys pushed a glass into my hand and filled it with champagne, and I saw Captain East, the Chaplain pushing his way through the crowd towards me.

"Good heavens, Mr Green, it's just like cup final day, I haven't seen so many people since I was in Delhi, have you been to Delhi yet?"

I said I had, but only for a day, and that I would be going later in the week.

"Ah yes, that will be to send the story about Frank, I expect."

"I may mention him, but the main story is about the British withdrawal from India."

And India's independance

"Come, come, Mr Green, you don't expect me to believe that, do you? I don't think a top flight reporter would be sent to a pokey little Indian village for that kind of story, Bombay or Calcutta yes, but

Ranpure, no. I think you are here to make something out of the boy Frank, you have obviously seen him and spoken to him, do you think he is the Son of God?"

I said, "yes, yes I do." No real harm could be done by admitting it now, there was not enough time for another newspaper man to get out here and find Frank and release the story before I did.

"Would you mind telling me why?"

I said, "there are several reasons really, the most important being Frank himself. There is something about him, about the way he talks he has an aura, he has an absolute and honest belief in himself, a purity that that I don't think could be faked could not be false, when you look in his eyes you see honesty and truth.

I met a man who had not used his arm since childhood, since an Ox trampled on it. Frank healed it, I don't know if that is a miracle by today's standards, but it must come pretty close to it. There was another man that Frank brought back from the dead, I haven't seen him, but they are simple people, they wouldn't make up things like that, and even if they did their stories would differ. Dozens of people saw the miracle and everyone I have spoken to tells the same story."

Another houseboy pushed by and filled our glasses. I could hear Jahmel shouting, "I haven't signed anything yet, but they have accepted my offer, and work will start on the Shrine as soon as the papers are signed."

The Chaplain said, "you know it's a funny thing, people like me, church men, we spend our lives teaching the ways of God, following examples set out in the bible, and believing them, and now something may have happened that the bible has told us will happen, that God shall come to the earth again, and we find it hard to believe. I personally am frightened and sceptical, I suppose the things that as a Man of God I shouldn't be."

I said, "the trouble is, you are a man first, and a Man of God second, and as a man you must realise that religion has lost its way. Jesus said that his Disciples should leave all their worldly goods and follow him with nothing and God would provide, and yet the Church is a wealthy organisation that pays its workers' wages, and Bishops live in palaces and concern themselves with politics." I said, "if you saw

Frank and you were completely convinced that he was the Son of God, what would you do?"

The Chaplain looked at me and said, "I would stay as close to him as possible and do all I could to help him."

I said, "well, I have heard him preach and one of the things he said was that there was no need for churches, that organised religion was wrong. Would you help him to pull down the very churches that you helped to build?"

"Yes, I would.

Well we will see, won't we." The Chaplain said. "Where is he now? I feel that I must find out as soon as possible."

"He is on the Plains of Lucknow, at a Cholera Camp, but I don't think he will be there long, the monsoons are due at any time and when the rains start there won't be much he can do, the whole area will be flooded. He may come back to the plantation or he may keep going. He says that he will travel the world preaching, he knows the major languages and plans to visit every country on the Earth preaching."

The Chaplain looked at me for a minute and said: "The plains of Lucknow cover a vast area, if I am going to find him I think I had better leave right away, don't you?" He handed me his glass and started to push his way through the crowd towards the front door then he stopped and shouted, "Thank you, Mr Green, thank you," then he started to push through the crowd again and I stood on tiptoe and shouted over the heads: "Good luck, Chaplain, I hope you find what you are looking for."

I was glad that somebody was going to make an effort to find out the truth for themselves. I felt lost now that Captain East had gone. I looked around for someone to talk to but they were busy with their own conversations, and I wasn't sure if they could speak English anyway, so I pushed my way into the bar towards Jahmel; he saw me coming and said:

"Come along, Arthur over here and I'll introduce you to some charming people." Mr and Mrs Granger and the Reverend Johnson they tried to look pleased to see me. There were two school teachers and a wealthy landowner, Dr Nazeem in the group and we talked the same sort of rubbish that's said at cocktail parties all over the world.

Several glasses of champagne later Jahmel looked at his watch and said, "I am afraid I have to leave you now, I've got one or two last minute things to see to."

I followed him, saying, "I would find Rhani and see if there was anything I could do to help." I pushed my way to the front door and looked up at the sky a Trillian stars twinkled in the black sky each one of them maybe a world like ours, with our joys and our sadness, and maybe another son of God.

I thought about the camp wondered how things were at the camp, what had happened to the little girl.? If the Captain had gone back or made up some story about the jeep breaking down. I looked at my watch, it was three o'clock, the procession would be starting soon and then maybe a music-less dance to follow that. What was left of the day looked as if it would be long and hot. I left the front door and walked down the long hall to the kitchen. I wanted to find Rhani and help, I knew that what she had said about us was true and I wanted to see if it made her sad as I felt. The kitchen was full, women and boys rushing about like the Keystone Cops, she was pointing here and pushing there, tasting this and - scrutinising that. She saw me, and I said, "Is there anything I can do to help?"

"Thank you, Arthur, but you will miss the procession."

"Well, that doesn't matter, processions were never my strong point, I've never even seen the Lord Mayor's Show."

She had just scooped a finger full of something that was being carried past her. She said between mouthfuls: "There are some wild blossom boughs on the floor of the ballroom, if you could sort out the decent flowers and cut them off we'll present them to the ladies later."

I was glad to be out of the way and have something to do. I went down the hall to the ballroom and opened the door, the smell of flowers hung in the room like an invisible fog, it was sweet and warm and thick. It reminded me of Kandy floss, the smell that drifted down the to tease impatient children, clutching pennies in their hands.

Long tables had been put along the far wall in front of the drawn curtains. There was an oil lamp alight at each end of the room which gave just enough light to see the fine linen and silver on the table. There was an ornate silver candelabra on each table surrounded by silver dishes and salvers and silver and glass goblets. I thought, things can't be too bad for Jahmel or he would have sold the silver. The branches were spread all over the floor, great boughs that were dying, pink and white and red blossoms. I found a knife and secateurs on a table and set about cutting off the sprays. When I had finished, and laid out the sprays on the tables around the room and threw the empty branches into the small garden I went along to the kitchen and washed my hands. The food was spilling off of every table and flat space in the kitchen. Large birds that looked like turkeys, suckling pigs with fresh fruit tumbling out of their open mouths and great glazed faces with cherry eyes watched me walk to the sink. The hustle and bustle was finished and only the head cook remained, specially hired for the Rain Feast. I told him how much I admired his culinary efforts, he nodded his head and said something in Indian. I nodded too and we both pretended we understood each other. How he had managed to prepare food like that on the prehistoric range in the Imperial kitchens I will never know. I went to the end of the hall past the stairway to the bar, it was empty and so was the hallway in front of it.

The front steps of the Imperial were packed with the Hotel guests and the noise of their clapping and laughter drifted down the hall. I walked to the front door and looked over their heads, the procession was in full swing. Both sides of the square were packed with people laughing and pointing at the Ox drawn carts as they came by, they rumbled past one after the other. The working carts had been covered with flowers even the Oxen had garlands of flowers around their necks. Each cart represented some facet of the farmer's work, Jute, Tea, Rice, Sugar and Tobacco. The one going by now had high sides, and a great Bull stood in the middle tied from either side. A small boy sat on the beast's back, he had an open umbrella over his head, the stem of it ran down his back and it was tied to him with string and bandage, to welcome the monsoon I suppose. His head was thrown back and he was laughing and laughing, the tears were running down his cheeks like rain, IT WAS THE LITTLE BEGAR BOY. I waved to him but he didn't see me, so I clapped instead and shouted with the others. The last float was an ornate cart covered in flowers with an enormous Budda on it, garlands of flowers hung down over his fat belly. Next was a late entry that caused even more interest than the Budda, it was an open Army jeep towing a small trailer, packed with soldiers, at the wheel was Sergeant Michael Jones.

They pulled up in front of the Imperial and the square grew silent. They jumped out and stood by the jeep, the steps were packed, there was no way up, they looked around the square at the silent crowds, looking unsure of themselves, uncertain what to do. I started to push my way through the crowd. The sight of a jeep load of British Soldiers wouldn't exactly put the Indian guests at ease, so I said: "Look, everyone it's the band, we'll have music tonight." I wasn't sure they all understood me but I kept saying, "The Band, music, music."

By the time I had reached the bottom of the steps they had realised what it was all about and some of them started clapping. The Sergeant's face burst into a smile when he saw me.

"Good evening, Sir, Sergeant Michael Jones and Light Infantry Ensemble reporting for duty as requested." There were five others and I shook hands with each of them and said in my best military voice: "I shall personally see to it that the Brigadier General knows that you men have voluntarily given up your weekend leave to play for him, I know he will appreciate it."

I led them up the steps, by the time we had got to the top the guests were calling out, "music, music", and we were being slapped on the back.

When we were in the Hotel I said: "Right, Sergeant, I think the first thing that is called for after that drive is a drink."

"Yes, Sir, it was a bit further than we thought, we expected to arrive at about lunchtime."

I didn't answer him but led them through into the bar. "Right lads what's it going to be? We will find you some Indian beer " Charley was behind the bar and I said: "Charley you must look after the gentlemen, they are not to pay for anything while they are in the Imperial. Now if you will excuse me, Sergeant, there are one or two things I must see to."

I left the bar and went to find Rhani. She was in the ballroom gathering up the sprays of blossoms that I had cut, and told her the band had arrived

"Oh, Arthur that's wonderful. What a relief, Have you told Jahmel?"

"No, but before I do- if they say anything about a Brigadier General just say that we're expecting him later. I told them one would be attending to get them here, then we can all act surprised when he doesn't show up."

She pretended to be annoyed, "Arthur Green that's downright deceitful."

"I know, but it was deceit or no music, anyway they won't know the difference when they've had a few drinks."

I left the ballroom and walked down the long hallway towards the bar. Jahmel was coming down the stairs.

"Ah, Green, any sign of your musical friends?" Jahmel was getting more pompous as he got used to his new position in the community, the soon to be owner of the Tea Plantation, and prosperous Hotel owner.

"Yes, I said, with a mock wiping of my brow, they have just arrived." He put on his friendly, I'm-one-of-the-boy's face.

"That's wonderful, Arthur, where are they?"

"They are in the bar. I told them as long as they were in the Imperial they could have whatever they liked," I added, "on the house". As he strode into the bar I made the introductions and during the next hour some serious drinking was done.

Jahmel looked at his watch, "Arthur, I think it's time we changed. Sergeant if your men would like to tune up we will see you later."

I took the Sergeant to the ballroom, while the others went out to the jeep and trailer to get their instruments. The tables beneath the windows were groaning with the weight of the food and all the oil lamps were alight. Sergeant Jones was impressed. The ballroom really did look very good.

There were so many guests they would obviously be sharing rooms to change in. As I reached the top of the stairs I saw Rhani going into one of the bedrooms, her arms full of blossom sprays. I went to my room and took the Napoleon uniform from the wardrobe and started to change. I was struggling with one of the boots when I heard a car door slam, it was not like a normal car door slamming, more of a swish and an expensive thud. I hobbled across to the window and looked out. Parked outside of the Hotel was a long shining Rolls Royce, on the other side of the square was an equally shining Mercedes, as I watched its lights were turned off and it melted into the shadows. A chauffeur was walking around the Rolls, he opened the rear door on the far side, somebody got out. His face was hidden by the top of the car, but I could see a black tie and dinner suit through the windows, he walked slowly around the back of the car and up the Hotel steps, looking suave and immaculate, was Jennah Ghats. Before I went downstairs I remembered thinking, I hope nobody tells Sergeant Michael Jones that Jannah Ghats is one of the leaders of the Mughal.

The moment I stepped outside the bedroom door I felt self-conscious, I stood there for a minute in my Napoleon uniform. Jennah Ghats was obviously not going to change, then one of the other bedroom doors opened and a man stepped out into the hall, he was dressed in rags carrying an 'iron' ball in his hand, a heavy looking iron chain ran from it to his ankle, and I felt better.

Jennah Ghats was seated at the end of the bar leaning against the wall. A freshly opened bottle of champagne and a half filled glass in front of him. He smiled into the mirror when he saw me and turned around slowly.

"Mr Green, I nearly didn't recognise you, the Napoleon uniform suits you admirably .I am sure you have many battles to win, but remember you lost the big one.

"Thank you, I hope that doesn't mean I'm a natural loser?"

"Certainly not, and anyway Napoleon was one of history's greatest winners until he met Wellington.".

"I shall just have to hope then that I get through tonight without meeting my particular Waterloo, won't I ?

Charley was doing something at the other end of the bar, he had entered into the spirit of things and had dressed up as a barman. Jennah Ghats rapped on the bar and said: "Another glass for Napoleon please. You will join me Mr Green, won't you?"

Charley brought the glass. As I climbed onto a bar stool next to Minister Ghats I could hear a wobbly trumpet playing 'Ain't Mis-Behaving' drifting up from the ballroom. I said, "I wasn't expecting to see you tonight, Mr Ghats, I didn't know you had been invited."

"I haven't exactly been invited, but Jahmel and I have been acquainted for some time and as his hospitality is renowned so I thought I might throw myself on his mercy. The news of the

Rain Feast's revival reached us in Delhi, it seemed too much of an opportunity to miss." He filled his glass with champagne. "I hope you enjoyed your visit to the Club, Mr Green, Elizabeth speaks of you highly and sends her," he paused, "regards I ignored his veiled reference,and drank my warm Champagne."

"Yes, thank you, it's not every day a humble reporter has the chance of staying at the celebrated Colonial Club and mixing with men who can guide a nation, and shape its future, it was indeed a most profitable meeting, I shall long keep the memory." As I finished speaking the thought came to me that once the full story was sent, the Mughal might not think it advisable to have someone floating about who knew that the Messiah was being promoted by a government minister and his cohorts.

Jannah Ghats was saying: "We will, of course, have the pleasure of your company again on Tuesday, won't we Mr Green?"

He said Tuesday slowly and deliberately. So that was to be D Day
. Ghats had stopped speaking and was staring into the mirror. Behind us dressed in a Gold edged Roman Toga with a Laurel Leaf Crown on his head, stood Jahmel, he looked very angry.

He snapped: "would you mind leaving us, Mr Green, the Minister and I have things to discuss .

I said, "Of course not," and picked up my drink and left the bar. The hall and stairway were empty so I leaned against the wall by the bar door and tried to hear what they were saying.

"What the bloody hell are you doing here, Ghats? I thought we had finished our business in Delhi."

"We had indeed, Jahmel don't worry. Your little secret will be safe with me, I have merely come to enjoy myself and to meet your charming sister, I have heard so much about her."

Little secret? what secret could Jahmel and Ghats have between them? Maybe Jahmel had borrowed the money for the plantation from the Minister.

I heard a bedroom door open upstairs and moved away quickly to the front door and looked out. The shining black Rolls Royce was still in front of the Hotel. I could hear more guests coming down the stairs talking and laughing, the wobbly trumpet was playing 'Sweet Sue' now

. When it was quiet again I turned around just in time to see Jahmel storm out of the bar and down the hall towards the ballroom. Shortly after that Jennah Ghats came out, he saw me at the front door and said, "Come along Mr Green, we will go and join in the fun shall we?" I followed him down to the ballroom and we went in.

The oil lamps had been turned down and the ballroom was in a soft half-light. Most of the couples were dancing and the rest were sitting at the tables around the floor. Sergeant Michael Jones' men were doing their best with 'How High the Moon'. Jahmel was standing by the food tables talking to the Sergeant, he hadn't taken his eyes off Jennah Ghats since we entered the room. The band comprised, Trumpet, Trombone, Clarinet, Drums and Piano, and played with a distinct ragtime flavour with Sergeant Jones featured on solo Public Relations. Jennah was being greeted from several parts of the room, and stopped to talk with a group below the band, so I made my way through the dancers to Jahmel and the Sergeant. Jahmel said, "Arthur I was just telling the Sergeant how much everybody was appreciating the music, a fine effort."

"Yes, indeed," I said, "it seems to be going very well."

The Sergeant said, "What time are you expecting the Brigadier General, Sir?"

I said, "Your men must be thirsty, Sergeant, if you would like to give me a hand we'll organise some chits."

The windows behind the food tables had been opened and a gentle breeze was billowing the heavy curtains, but the ballroom was packed and very hot. As we started to cross the dance floor, the door opened and Rhani came in, the wobbly trumpet went even more wobbly and a quiet fell over the ballroom. She was dressed as a Grecian Goddess in a low cut simple white dress tied loosely at the waist. Her black hair was plaited with small white flowers and fell softly over her shoulders, she looked like everyman's dream of the most beautiful girl in the world, as if she had just strolled down from Mount Olympus. She stood there for a moment surveying her kingdom.

I started to cross the ballroom towards her, but Jennah Ghats was already at the bottom of the steps holding out his hand to her, she smiled and took his hand and stepped down onto the dance floor. He took her in his arms and they started to dance as the Light Infantry Ensemble broke into 'A Pretty Girl is Like a Melody'.

I said, "Come on, Sergeant, let's see about those bloody drinks."

The bar was still empty, I asked Charley for a bottle of scotch and two glasses. The Sergeant said: "You looked pretty angry in there, is she your girl or something?"

"No, not even or something now, it's a long story, Serge and the villain is 8,000 miles."

"Well, I think that smarmy git in there is taking liberties and you ought to give him a right hander anyway."

I laughed and said, "That smarmy git happens to be a Government Minister, and there is a Mercedes parked in the shadows across the square that's sure to have two or three bodyguards in it who are here to see that nobody gives him a right hander."

The Sergeant topped up our glasses and said, "it's the same everywhere mate, at least you'll be going home soon, that's something, we'll be stuck out here for God knows how long." He ordered the drinks for the band, put them on a tray and left the bar.

I sat there for an hour drinking, I didn't want to watch Rhani with Jennah Ghats. I was joined occasionally by a King and Queen or French Nobleman but mostly the bar was empty except for me. The music stopped and shortly after that the musicians with Sergeant Jones came into the bar. They ordered drinks, large ones, and the Sergeant said: "You should see her now, mate, he hasn't left her all evening, smarmy git."

Then Jahmel came into the bar, he sat away from me at the far end of the counter. He looked furious, and said, "they are starting to eat now, Green, you had better get some food while you can."

The scotch had taken the edge off my appetite, and anyway I didn't like being called 'Green', so I didn't answer him. The band was having a great time, unlimited free drink was all they could have hoped for, they seemed to have forgotten about the Brigadier General. After a while they drifted back into the ballroom and gave us a version of 'Tiger Rag' that not even Fred Astaire could have danced to. I wondered how the townspeople were celebrating the Rain Feast, after all it was they that were really interested in the rain. I remembered the little beggar boy balancing on the back of the bull, he would be with his friends now and this was one day that he would be treated as normal. I left the bar and wandered out into the square, they were at the end of the square where the lane runs down to the plantation road. They were around a great bonfire dancing and singing. The reflection from the flames danced on the polished parked cars. I could see two men sitting in the front of the Mercedes. One of them was an Indian, the other looked like a Negro. I walked down the steps past the Rolls towards the fire, some of the townspeople recognised me and called me as I drew near. They still thought I was here to buy land for the Hotel, The Ranpure Hilton, they would be disappointed, but if Jahmel's idea came true about people flocking to the Shrine, they would be better off anyway. The floral cart with the Budda on it was on the other side of the fire, in the glow from the fire he looked as if he were laughing, maybe he knew something we didn't. A smiling, laughing girl caught hold of my arm and I was one of them whirling and dancing around the fire. When we stopped I saw Achmed standing with Ravi, they were pointing at me and laughing. I went over to them glad of the chance to rest. Ravi saluted and Achmed said, "You are a natural dancer, Mr Green, you must have some native blood in you."

I said, "You might be right about the native blood but that's not what they said about my dancing at the Hammersmith Palais." He didn't understand and I couldn't be bothered to explain. "Where is the boy, the little beggar boy?"

Achmed said, "He was here a little while ago, but he is sad when he sees the dancing, he has probably gone home."

I left them and went to the little alley way I had seen him come out of. If he had only just left, he couldn't have gone far, he didn't move very fast. There he was in the shadows wriggling along in the dust. I ran down the alley behind him and picked him up. I put my hand under his armpits and lifted him into my arms. I carried him back to where Achmed and Ravi stood. The boy's great brown eyes were full of tears and they were falling down his cheeks. He was very dusty and the tears had washed his cheeks clean. I said to Achmed, "I want to tell him a story, will you translate for me?" He nodded. I said, "About 50 years ago a little boy was born in a French Village, something like Ranpure, his father was a Count and his family were very important. They hoped that when the little boy grew up he would be a great man, an important man to carry on the family tradition. One day the little boy had an accident and he hurt his spine, his legs never grew anymore. His family took him to all the best doctors in the world but nobody could help him, his legs stayed the size of a little boy's legs for the rest of his life . His father stopped loving him because he would never grow up to be like him."

"The little boy was very unhappy. One day he started painting, when his father saw him, which was not often he looked at the boy's painting and said: "It was rubbish," but the boy kept painting the way he wanted to. When he was old enough he left home and went to live in Paris where all the great painters lived. He was very poor and it was harder for him because he had been used to having whatever he wanted. People laughed at him because he was so small, and they laughed at his paintings, but he kept doing what he wanted to, and painting the way he wanted to and by the time he died in 1901, only forty-six years ago, the people who understood about art had recognised his talent and understood him. So you see it is important not to lose hope. Now millions of people know his story and realise how hard life had been for him and that he was a real genius."

I looked at them and they looked at me. I wondered if the boy had understood, if any of them had understood. The others were dancing around the fires again. I lifted the boy onto my shoulders and said to Achmed: "Tell him I am going to give him a dancing lesson," and I danced off into the crowd as Achmed shouted to the boy. The girls took it in turns to dance with me around the fire, holding my shoulders and looking at the boy as if they were dancing with him. I could feel the boy bouncing and laughing on my shoulder. I danced until I was ready to drop, then sat the boy still laughing next to the Budda.

The fire was dying now and we could see over it the entrance to the Imperial. Jahmel was leading the guests down the steps into the square, they were carrying boxes, they set the boxes down and started to take out the fireworks Jahmel had said he would get. Rhani was standing with Jenneh Ghats at the top of the steps, as I watched them he walked down the steps and across to the Mercedes and said something to the driver and he drove the car around the corner out of sight. As he walked back across the square a rocket whooshed up into the sky and exploded into a hundred tiny stars. In the light of the rocket I could see Ghats say something to Rhani and they both laughed. The dancing had stopped now and everyone was watching the fireworks. I left then and walked quietly around the square in the shadows to the Hotel, behind Rhani and Ghats into the Imperial. It was empty inside, I went straight to my room, took off the Napoleon uniform and got into bed. I pulled the mosquito net down and lay there thinking about Rhani in the distance I could hear the band playing. The light from the fireworks danced on the ceiling of my room. I made up my mind then, that when I had the rest of the story on Frank I would go home. It didn't matter if I got the sack, if Bill Steel didn't like it he could do the other thing. I had the rubies now.

When I awoke on Sunday morning I had that feeling, the feeling I had when I was a kid and we had gone for a week's holiday to Clacton and stayed in some crumby guest house. It was raining and I sat in a tatty lounge looking out of the window across a Ludo board at the rain. I felt I was missing something, and I didn't know what., I had the same feeling now, but this time I knew what I was missing.

Jennah Ghats had hovered between Rhani and I like a black cloud. I already knew that there was no future for us now she had gone so easily to Ghats.

I had two days to go, but that still left today and Monday. There was a knock at the door and Charley came in. "Good morning, sir, did you enjoy the party?"

"Yes, thank you, what's happening downstairs?" He started running my bath. "Nobody is about yet, sir, just as well as there is a lot of cleaning up to be done, some of the guests only went to bed an hour ago."

"I came to bed after the fireworks, I thought things were starting to break up then."

"Oh no, sir, the band moved into the bar, sir. Some of the guests went to bed then but the rest carried on the party in the bar, sir. I think it was our most successful Rain Feast."

"Have the band gone?"

"No, sir, the Sergeant was in rather a bad way, he kept saying he had to stay and meet a Brigadier General, he collapsed in the dining room on the floor, they carried him to the Billiard room, he's still there. The rest of the musicians are scattered throughout the various rooms, on the floor."

I said, "What about Rhani?"

"She was one of the last to leave, sir. She went to bed about an hour ago, soon after Minister Ghats left."

"And Jahmel?"

"He is still downstairs, sir. He decided he would spend what was left of the night on the billiard table he and the sergeant were head to tail on the billiard table,."

Charley started to leave. "There is just one thing, sir, the Sergeant has one of our silver salt pots in his pocket, I am sure someone put it there for a joke. Perhaps you would remind him of it before he leaves." Charley left the room and I took my bath.

Downstairs it looked like one of those scenes we've seen too much of in London, it looked like the blitz. One of the soldiers, I think it was the trombone player was asleep on the stairs and anyone going up or down had to step over him. Someone else was laying across two chairs in the hall, his head on the desk by the front door. There was litter everywhere, streamers and paper hats, crumpled serviettes and broken blossoms, half-filled glasses and pieces of food trodden into the carpet. Charley and his men were running about like stretcher bearers. Things seemed to have got drastically out of hand after my departure. The Sergeant still lay on the billiard table like a felled tree and Jahmel with him.. The houseboys were cleaning up and laying the tables around the room,. I took the salt pot from his the sergeant's pocket, put it on a table in the dining room and sat down, wishing it was Tuesday.

I felt bad about sitting there expecting breakfast in the middle of all that mess, but at least I hadn't helped to create it. I wondered how Mr and Mrs Granger and the Reverend had got on, it didn't look like their sort of party, but you never can tell. After a while, not too long really considering, a boy appeared with a pot of tea and some toast. I had just poured the tea when the oak panelled billiard room door slowly opened. Jahmel stood in the doorway, somehow his laurel leaf crown had got around his neck and his Toga had become separated from the top half of his body and hung from his waist like a skirt. The houseboys stopped work and stared at him, we all stopped and stared at him, except the Sergeant who loomed behind him, He stood there for a moment working out his route across the dining room and then set out,. he walked like James Cagney does when somebody has filled him full of lead. Having crossed the dining room with only minor mishaps he disappeared into the hall, the sergeant behind him.

I finished my breakfast and left the Hotel. I was in the way and I didn't particularly want to be told what a great party I had missed. Things were normal in the square. The traders were starting the day's business and the sun was starting to get hot, the sky was clearing, no sign of the rain clouds. The little beggar boy was not in his usual spot.

Achmed called to me from across the square and I went to meet him. "Good morning, Arthur, I did not think we would see you so early today, the party was very late."

"The party was, but I wasn't, I went to bed when I left you.

There looks like a lot of clearing up to do, Put me to work Achmed,. we walked back into the hotel he produced a couple of aprons and. we worked steadily until late morning, picking up, putting back, finding homes for lost candle sticks and lamps, and anything that looked out of place. Clearing up the party's detritus We were taking a well-earned rest when Achmed turned to me with a smile and said

You will come to my home, my wife will make us Chapattis and then I will drive you to where ever you wish."

It seemed like a good idea, so I followed Achmed out into the sunlight and across the square, we walked down the lane to the Plantation Road, it was busy but not as busy as before. then turned right away from the Plantation and drove down a track that ran behind the field with the stable. At the bottom of the track I saw the old Mercedes in front of a large brick house. There was a bamboo canopy jutting from the front. The Mercedes was beneath it in the shade. Next to the car at a table sat Ravi, he jumped up when he saw us and ran to meet us shouting. A woman came to the door wiping her hands on a cloth. Ravi stopped in front of us and saluted and gave me that same toothless grin he had when we first met. Achmed put his arm around the old man and we all walked towards the house.

Achmed said, "You have made a real friend of my father, Arthur.

"I should have guessed that Ravi was Achmed's father, they were never far apart. Achmed's wife was a female version of Achmed, happy and round and smiling. She told me through Achmed that her husband and father-in-law had told her all about me and that I was very welcome. We sat at the table beneath the canopy while she got us some cool lemonade to drink. We sat there in the shade, as the day slowly got hotter the flies and mosquitos chased each other. In the distance I could see the great Mango Tree that shaded the stable. On the other side of the track open fields stretched away to a small patch of trees in the distance. It was very peaceful and I was glad to be there.

Ravi told us stories of when he was a Ghurkha soldier and fought for the British in Bengal. Achmed had translated and added a bit to each story. At about mid-day Achmed's wife presented us with a great plateful of Chapatti's and some stew.. Ravi told his stories more and more slowly and Achmed made them more and more fantastic until one by one we fell asleep.

When I awoke the main part of Sunday was over, it was evening and cooler. The sun had gone behind the trees and was casting long shadows across the fields. Achmed and Ravi were gone and I sat there alone listening to the drone of the insects as they made their way home. I got up and went into the house. Achmed's wife greeted me and with the aid of sign language she joked about my falling asleep, but what with the trip to Delhi and the Lucknow Plains, and the party I needed it. Then she told me with the same language that Achmed and Ravi had gone, she wanted me to stay for more food and tea, but my sleep had made me even more tired and I wanted to get back to the Imperial and go to bed and finish with Sunday. I could write the despatch tomorrow and get ready to leave India. We said our goodbyes and I walked slowly down the track that led to the Plantation Road. The evening smells were hanging in the air, cooking, crops, and flowers, dung and smoke all mixing with the late evening warmth. The clouds were gathering on the horizon. I crossed the road and walked through the back street of Ranpure to the Imperial.

There was no sign of the aftermath of the party and the bodies were gone, the Hotel had got back its look of decaying dignity. There were one or two irremovable scars but Jahmel would capitalise on them in years to come. That stain or that cigarette burn would lead to an evening's discussion of the revival of the Rain Feast. They might even be graded as a vintage. Ah yes, 47 was a great year.

Jahmel called to me from the bar as I paused. "Green, Green, come along in old chap, been out?"

He had obviously slept very late himself because he didn't know I had been out all day. "A hair of the dog, what!"

The bar was empty except for Jahmel and Charley. Jahmel called for a bottle of Champagne: "The best thing for a hangover, old boy." I didn't feel like explaining that I didn't have a hangover and why, so I took the glass. I was getting to like warm Champagne

"What a night, Arthur, I ended up on the billiard table and the band have only just left."

It was starting already, the descriptions of the party, they would be pretty accurate because I had been there, but with each telling they would gain something. To shut him up I said, "I was surprised to see Jennah Ghats here."

He reacted like a real professional: "Surprised! surprised old chap, he was invited, he's an old friend."

I said, "Is he an old friend of Rhani's too?"

"No, he is a business acquaintance. Rhani had heard of him of course, but she hadn't met him. As you know he is a Government Minister, it does us good to have people like that down here." The dinner gong rang and we took our glasses into the dining room. Like the rest of the Hotel it had been cleaned up and the extra tables had been removed.

Rhani was already seated at our table, she smiled: "Did you have a good time last night, Arthur? I didn't see much of you."

I felt like saying, "It's a wonder you saw anything except Jennah Ghats," but I said: "I had enjoyed myself and spent my time making sure I didn't meet my Waterloo.

Dinner was a quiet affair, we were all tired, when we were finished Jahmel made a half-hearted suggestion that we played snooker. I excused myself saying that I needed an early night.

Monday, felt like the other days that I had awoken to in that oak filled bedroom, but it was different, if I could get a seat on a plane tomorrow, it would be my last day. The thought of Fleet Street and the Nags Head, bacon sandwiches at Mick's made it seem like a good day.

Charley knocked and came into the room. "Good morning, Sir, did you sleep well?"

"Yes, thank you, Charley. What's the weather like? any sign of rain?"

"Yes, Sir, I think the rain will come today or tomorrow for sure."

"Well I hope it waits until I have gone."

"You leaving, Sir?"

"Yes. I am going tomorrow morning, first thing. If you see Achmed today will you tell him I want to see him. I want to make an early start and catch the first available plane tomorrow night."

Charley started to run the bath then came back into the bedroom. "I am sure we will all be sorry to see you leave, Sir, we have had good times in the Imperial again while you have been here."

"Well don't worry, Charley, Jahmel has some plans for the old place. You may soon be wishing the quiet old days were back."

Charley walked to the window and looked out, "The rains will come soon now, Sir, and if they come before tomorrow morning you will not be able to leave. The roads around Ranpure are only dirt tracks, a car could never travel on them once the monsoon starts, it is alright once you are on the Delhi Road, but you could not leave Ranpure in the monsoon."

"Great, that's all I need;" if I didn't show up in Delhi to send that despatch on Tuesday all Jennah Ghats carefully laid plans would backfire. He had bought himself £10,000 worth of Insurance. He would be pleased. I had to get there somehow even if I swam. I got out of bed and got a pound note from my coat. I gave it to Charley and said: "Can you get a message to Achmed right away?"

"Yes, Sir, I'll send one of the boys."

"Well, tell him to get here as soon as he can, I want to go to Delhi now."

Charley put the note in his pocket and said: "I'll see to it at once, you can count on me. Achmed will be here in less than an hour."

As soon as Charley had gone I had a quick bath and shave. I got dressed and threw my few belongings into my bag. I didn't know anyone else who would go to India with one suit, three shirts and three pairs of pants and socks. The Major's uniform still hung in the wardrobe with the crossed belts and gun. They would find them when they cleaned the rooms. I went downstairs, left my bag in the hall and went out onto the steps to wait for Achmed. It was still early and I would wait until he came to say my goodbyes. The Square was starting to live again as the traders set out their produce. They knew me now and waved as they worked. It was a dull morning there were clouds in the sky, white clouds, they didn't look like rain clouds but they were there. Somebody tapped me on the shoulder, it was Charley. "I'm sorry, Sir, but Achmed is away on business and he won't be back until this evening."

I was stunned, I was so keyed up to be going right away that Charley's words hit me like a sledgehammer. So that was that, I had to wait now.

Charley said: "A message was left at his house to come to the Imperial as soon as he returned."

He went back into the Hotel. I looked up into the sky again. They were only white clouds; the rain would probably hold off for a day or two, I went back into the Hotel and tried to believe it. Jahmel was standing by my bag, when he saw me he said. "Off Green?" I wasn't quite sure whether he was asking me or telling me, so I grunted. He made me feel as if I were skipping out of the back door with the Hotel towels under my arm and my pockets full of ash trays. He wasn't too happy with my response so he said: "Are you leaving us, Arthur?"

I said, "I was, but I am not now. I was hoping to leave before the rains broke, but Achmed is out of town."

"Well, I could have told you that, dear boy, if you had only asked, he's running a little errand for me. Now why don't you take your bag back to your room while I order breakfast."

I picked up my bag and went up the stairs. I could feel his eyes on me, I did'nt know why but I had the feeling he did'nt want me to leave.

When I came back into the dining room Rhani was at the table. Jahmel was reading a week old copy of World News. Rhani looked up: "Jahmel tells me you were planning to leave Arthur?"

"Yes, I thought if I left right away I would beat the rain. I was waiting until the last minute to say goodbye so as not to disturb you, but Achmed is out of town so I will have to wait until tomorrow and take my chance."

"Well, today will be an anti-climax for you then, but we will try to think of some way to keep you amused while we have breakfast."

I sat down as a houseboy brought in the food. Jahmel said: "What had you planned to do today, Green?"

"I had no plans I was hoping to be on my way, but I think I will do some more work on my story about Frank."

Jahmel poured the tea and said, "Good, you may use my study. I have quite a good collection of books too, you may care to do some reading."

I said, "that I would appreciate the use of the study." We finished breakfast in silence. Jahmel read the World News and Rhani seemed preoccupied, and distant.

Jahmel's study was oak panelled and dusty. One wall was covered with shelves and packed with books. There were various animal heads around the room and by the window was a gun rack that carried about half a dozen rifles. I got my notes from my bedroom and went back into the study. I knew exactly what I wanted to say and it came easily. It wasn't hard to write about Frank; my only worry was that my story should be worthy of him. The study was at the back of the Hotel and it was very quiet.

At about mid-day I went to my bedroom and rested for a couple of hours until the hottest part of the day had passed, then returned to the study to finish the story. When it was finished I was pleased with it, very pleased, it said everything, it was a positive statement of what I believed. It would be the most important dispatch ever sent to a newspaper. Jennah Ghats had got his money's worth. There was a knock on the door and Charley came in with a pot of tea. He set it on the desk and said: "I'm afraid there is no sign of Achmed yet, Sir, but he will come to you as soon as he returns. The clouds have passed the rain will not come today."

"Thank you, Charley, and when you see him will you tell him that I must leave at first light in the morning."

"Yes, Sir I will tell him." Charley left the room and I read through the story again.

I had just finished my bath when the dinner gong rang. I dressed and went downstairs for my last evening at the Imperial. Jahmel and Rhani were in the Bar, they had just opened a bottle of Champagne to celebrate. Rhani looked more beautiful than ever, cool and distant and beautiful. Jahmel seemed very happy and was quite friendly, he called me Arthur.

Dinner was a very polite affair we were all on our best behaviour. Jahmel drank very little, saying he wanted to make sure that he had breakfast with me the next morning.

When dinner was finished Rhani said goodnight and goodbye, she hoped I had had a pleasant stay and that I enjoyed my trip to India, she shook hands with me as if I were a visiting cousin. Jahmel tapped me on the back and said: "I'll see you in the morning, Arthur, early to bed, early to rise, what!" and that was that.

Tuesday, Charley woke me before the sun was up, the room was filled with a dusky half-light as he ran my bath, then he went downstairs to organise some breakfast. And I bathed and dressed quickly, eager to get going. I took the rubies from my bag and put them in my pocket. I could just see the Customs Officer raiding my bag then holding up the leather pouch and saying, "What's this?"

Charley came back into the room and started to put my few belongings into my bag. When the bag was packed and as I was ready to leave he went to the window to give me a weather report on the monsoon, he said: "The rain will come soon now, Sir, it is a good thing that you are leaving right away." As he was turning away from the window he said, "Frank is back from the Lucknow Plains."

I went to the window and looked out into the dark square and said: "What makes you think that?"

"I have just seen Majid crossing the square, Sir, he is never far from the Messiah." Frank must have returned to the bungalow.

I went downstairs to breakfast thinking about Frank and how much I wanted to see him again to ask him about the little girl, but I had to leave, everything was arranged, perhaps there would be another time when I could ask him.

. Jahmel was waiting for me in the dining room. He got up when he saw me and said: "So the big day is here at last, Achmed will be here shortly, you will leave as soon as we have had breakfast." He seemed as pleased that I was going as I was. A houseboy brought the breakfast in on a tray. As I helped myself to the hot toast, Jahmel poured the tea and said, "I can remember getting up at this time at Cambridge and earlier, we would be going off to get into mischief, a small adventure of some sort." He smiled to himself as if remembering some forgotten joke. The prospect of the homeward journey had put me in a good mood and I felt that I should make some effort to make our last meeting a pleasant one.

I said, "What were you reading at Cambridge?"

He sipped his tea and said; "Modern languages."

I stopped and looked at him, that little one per cent of doubt had turned into a ball and was bouncing into the dark corners of my mind, it was touching sensitive nerves of memory and lighting the dark corners like the magnetised ball on a pinball machine... Click, the first night, Rhanhi had said: "Mr Green, we have both been looking forward to your visit for so long." So long? ... 200 Points. Click. I was surprised when Majid left, Sir. Jahmel made sure he only had the easy jobs to do. He always had plenty of money ... 200 Points ... Click ... "What languages do you speak? ... French, German, Spanish, Russian and Chinese ... 200 Points... Modern Languages ... Click. The ball bounced into the darkest corner of all. I remembered when I had first seen Frank, I had an overpowering feeling of recognition ... Click ... Jackpot. It was Jahmel that I recognised in Frank, I had been tricked, conned, had – somehow ... but how? The little ball stopped rolling and my mind went blank. There was one question, one last question I had to ask Frank. I hadn't thought of it before; it was too obvious. I jumped up and my chair tilted over and crashed to the floor, the noise of it echoing around the room.

Jahmel said, "Arthur, what's wrong? what's wrong?" as I ran from the room

. As I ran out into the deserted square I could hear him. "Come back, Arthur, don't be a bloody fool, forget it! forget it!"

As I ran down the lane to the Plantation Road it was packed with pilgrims again, even this early. They must have heard that Frank had returned. I pushed through them and across the field to the stable. The small boy heard me and ran from his hut and saddled a horse for me.

I dug my heels into the beast hard and galloped across the field to the road in a cloud of dust. As I rode down the Plantation Road I kept shouting to clear the crowds. By the time I reached the Lower Road the horse was white with sweat. The crowd was thicker here, spilling over from the clearing. I spurred the horse through, knocking them aside. I rode around the clearing through the trees and stopped behind the bungalow, then forced my way to the front and up the steps. I opened the front door and went in. It was empty, after all that, had Charley been wrong? I ran across the lounge to Frank's room and opened the door. Frank was lying on the bed, he looked up as I came in, he looked terrible. His white robe was covered with mud and sweat and blood, and there were dark rings around his eyes. He tried to smile when he saw me, but he was too weak, his head sunk back onto the bed. I knelt beside him and said; "Just one more question, Frank, I need your help then you can rest. What about Jahmel? It must have made things much easier for you having a man like Jahmel to help you. He must have been a father to you.

He looked at me with great tired sad eyes and said, "Jahmel? I do not know a Jahmel."

I said, "Rhani's brother, he has done a great deal to help you, he has been to all the surrounding districts to tell the people about you."

He sank back onto the bed and closed his eyes and said, "Rhani has no brother."

So there it was, what I had expected. I stood up - Frank was already asleep. I left the bungalow and stood on the veranda and looked out at the crowds. I didn't see Jahmel right away, he was standing half way between the bungalow and the Burning Hill in a clump of trees, a horse was tethered nearby. He stood in the shadows watching me. When I saw him he shouted something across the crowds, but I couldn't hear, then he waved something above his head. I could see what that was, it was a heavy powerful looking rifle. I automatically ran down the steps and started to push my way through the crowds away from him. It was like being in a sea, a sea of bodies. I pushed and punched my way through them like a mad man. I could hear his shouting all the time. I had to get out of the crowd away from the road and onto the open countryside. I would have a chance there, he was older than I was and carrying a heavy rifle, that would slow him down. Jahmel was in the thick of the crowd behind me now, so I pushed my way to the side of the road and started running through the tea bushes towards the Burning Hill. He wouldn't shoot me down in front of all these people and now I was over the brow of the Burning Hill I would have a chance.

As I ran across the Burning Hill the first fingers of sunlight ran across the sky and I saw a great black monsoon cloud just a few hundred feet high. All the time I ran I was expecting to hear the crack of the rifle, but there was no sound, nothing, except my pushing through the bushes. I ran down the hill and onto the flat land and across a field towards a clump of trees in the direction of Ranpore, through the trees and into the next field. In the far corner an Ox was standing watching me, I ran towards it, then stopped beside the beast and looked back, there was no sign of Jahmel. I leaned against a low wall gasping for breath, the sweat was running from me and soaking my suit. There was a little click in the distance and a red patch appeared between the beast's eyes, and it sank down onto its knees. The blood ran down its long face and dripped from the end of its nose into the dust. then it slumped over at my feet sending up a puff of dust.

I leaped over the low wall and down into a monsoon ditch and started to run around the field. I went from ditch to ditch, field to field towards Ranpore until I came to the stable, then I cut off left through the trees towards Achmed's house. There was just a chance that he would still be there, he was, the old Mercedes was parked in front of the old house. I pushed my way through the trees past the old car and fell into the house. I couldn't speak, I fell down on a bench and gasped for breath. Achmed and Ravi were sitting together talking. Achmed's wife was cooking, they all stared at me. As soon as I was able I gasped: "It's a trick, Jahmel has tricked us, he has tricked everyone. Frank has been set up by Jahmel somehow. I don't know how, I can't explain, but you must believe me. He is coming here now he has chased me from the Plantation, he is going to kill me. I know the truth."

Achmed said something to Ravi then jumped up and said: "I think now is a very good time to leave for Delhi, don't you, Arthur?" He ran out of the house, I started to follow him when I heard the rifle again. Achmed was just climbing into the car when the bullet hit him. The power of it sent him diving through the windscreen. I grabbed Ravi as he ran past me and threw him across the table, into the wall. I couldn't explain to him that he would be shot too if he went out. I ran through the house and out through the window at the back. I doubled back and ran along the ledge that led to the Plantation Road. I didn't hear the gun this time, but I felt it. I was hurled over with the power of the bullet and lay in the dust while the pain in my left shoulder grew bigger and bigger. It was then that I remembered the Browning, the Major's gun hanging in the wardrobe, if I could get that I still had a chance. I pushed myself to my feet and forced myself to run down to the end of the hedge pushing the pain out of my head, and across the crowded Plantation Road and through the back streets of Ranpore to the Imperial.

As I staggered up the steps I could feel the warm sticky blood running down my back. My shoulder felt on fire, every step sent the pain jolting through me. I pushed myself up the stairway and along the hall to my bedroom. I fell across the room to the wardrobe and pulled open the door, it was still there. I reached in and grabbed the holster, then I heard Rhani say: "I think we had better wait for Jahmel don't you, Arthur?"

I turned around slowly, Rhani was standing in the doorway, in her hand was a neat chrome plated ladies' gun and it was pointing at me. I stood looking at the gun and tried to work it out. Jahmel and Rhani, had they set up the boy? was she in it with them? I had heard about Americans being sold the Tower of London or Westminster Abbey, but this was the greatest confidence trick of all. A confidence trick to fool the World.

Black blasphemy on a grand scale. I was feeling sick and I leaned back against the wardrobe and closed my eyes. So Rhani had smiled sweetly and I had followed her into the black cavern of deception.

Achmed was dead, fat, laughing Achmed who had been a friend to me with more than words and it seemed that I was soon to follow him. I wasn't afraid of dying any more than I was afraid of being born but I had hoped that my life would at least run its natural course. I sensed Jahmel rather than heard him. I opened my eyes and Rhani was already looking out of the window when we heard his heavy running footsteps cross the square and enter the Hotel, then clump slowly along the hall and up the stairs. He would see Rhani in the doorway, there would be no gained time while he went from room to room looking for me.

How could a man charge around the countryside with a rifle killing a man, and hunting another and not arouse some interest, some concern. Surely someone would have reported it. But to whom? There was no friendly Bobby on the corner to run to. We had been too far away from the pilgrims when the shooting occurred, and the townspeople if they knew of it would probably say nothing. What little money came into the Town came through Jahmel and the Imperial. That left Achmed's wife and Ravi to raise the alarm, to get help.

Jahmel was breathing heavily, he looked at me with a disgust and contempt that he made no effort to hide. Finally, he said, "So, Mr Arthur, smart Alec Green thought he could spoil everything, did he? Did you really think that a little upstart from the East End educated at some back street slum school could outsmart me? The trouble with you, old chap is that you don't recognise a great opportunity when you see it. You had the chance, in spite of your humble beginnings of becoming the most famous reporter in history, of being rich and successful. That is the fundamental difference, Arthur between you and a gentleman. A gentleman would have recognised the opportunity and taken it. But because you have no breeding you were unable to recognise the things that a gentleman is taught from birth to covet, and so your inferiority has led, as it had to, to your demise."

Jahmel raised the barrel of the heavy hunting rifle towards me. I had to keep him talking somehow, long enough for the Market Square to get busy, then he might think twice about firing the gun. The pain was searing and the blood was dripping slowly from my hand like the steady beat of a metronome.

I said, "Now that things are a little clearer to me I must say that it was the most brilliantly conceived and executed plan, how on earth did you manage it?"

He seemed pleased and said: "As you will soon be leaving us to join your fathers nothing will be lost by telling you, although it may be a little too deep for you. I will try to keep it simple so that you can understand. It is brilliant, and it deserves telling.

When I have told you, you will be the only person on earth to know. Contrary to your obvious conclusions, Rhani does not know, although it is now time that she did."

I was feeling sick again and weak. I leaned back against the wardrobe. Jahmel said: "You had better sit down, Mr Green, you will need your powers of concentration."

I sat in a chair by the window. I put my handkerchief against the open wound in my back and pressed it in place with the chair. If it was a long story I wouldn't hear the end of it. I would die from loss of blood and Jahmel wouldn't have to use the rifle. All he had to do was stand there and watch me bleed to death. I hoped he didn't realise it.

"The whole thing really started by accident," said Jahmel. "About fifteen years ago, I had what you would call an affair with a young girl whilst on hols. She was, although very beautiful, the daughter of a farm labourer who had just come to the area looking for work. I employed the girl here at the Imperial for a short time. You may remember her, Rhani?"

Rhani looked as if she were going to speak then thought better of it. Jahmel continued. "It was the impetuosity of youth that guided me to her bed. The result of our union was that she became pregnant. When I knew her condition I sent her away to a village about twenty miles away to have the child. The declining trade of the Imperial had until that time caused me a great deal of concern. But when the young lady concerned produced twin boys I conceived a plan so brilliant that only I would be capable of bringing to fruition. I struck a bargain with the girl. If she would hand over one of the boys to my care and support and raise the other boy herself I would give her an allowance. She was also to tell no one I was the father, and she must stay in this area. She had been nursed by an ageing widow and I arranged that she would help raise my boy.

This then was the arrangement that the mother would have one son to live with her in this area, and that the widow should raise my son. There is a place not far from here that you may have heard of, Rhani will certainly know it, called the Place of the Gods." Rhani nodded. "The local people are afraid to go there; they think the Gods live there. It is a dense forest like a jungle. I built a house there in the trees, a great house with rooms and corridors. I cut away trees above it in the centre so that the sun would reach it. It was not easy to build a house there for the trees are close together and very thick, but with the help of some local craftsmen we managed, and when it was ready I took the boy and the old woman there, to the house, of course there were rumours about the Place of the Gods, but the people were superstitious and afraid to go near.. As soon as the boy was old enough I started to teach him all I knew, fortunately he had inherited my academic brilliance and he learned quickly. I also told him that we were special, chosen, and direct descendants of God and that as the Son of God he would one day do down to the Earth and shape its future. I taught him that he was in a place between Heaven and Earth.

"I went each day with food and to give him lessons, that is why I bought the house and built the stable so that I had a good excuse to be gone from the Hotel for a few hours each day riding. I taught the boy everything I knew academically, and also the things that would have to be like second nature to him if people were to believe he was really the Son of God. About goodness and kindness and humility. I taught him my own ideas about religion, about the stupidity of the caste system and the futility of the Temples."

I said, "How did you arrange about the miracles?"

"I met Majid at about the same time that I conceived the plan. He came here looking for work. I told him I would give him work for as long as he wanted it, that he would have extra money and security, but that in return he would cease to use one arm. At first I strapped the arm to his body beneath his shirt until it grew thin and useless. He had to tell everybody that it had been damaged when he was a child and it had been lifeless since then."

"What about the man who was brought back from the dead?"

"An epileptic. I relied on the gullibility of the peasants and their own eagerness to convince themselves of what they wanted to believe. I had no control over the movements of, I shall call my wife, to make things easier. It was essential that I should have no contact with her and that no one should know of our association, but as things turned out I could not have planned her movements or actions to be greater value to myself. When she found herself without my support or the help of the widow, she went to the Plantation of the Rising Moon to seek work. She was taken in by the Wilson's and she stayed there until with the most profound sense of decency she died. Of course, she didn't know it but she had obliged me immensely by dying, apart from the old widow, who was locked in the forest of the Gods, she was the only other person that knew of the existence of a twin boy to be her own son. So the stage was set, it was up to me now to produce a God. To take an ordinary mortal and instil in him such a belief in himself, such an absolute certainty that he was indeed a God, that he would make others believe it. That is how the years were spent, the long years of waiting. Having conducted this experiment and brought it to its natural conclusion, it is my belief that if a child is kept in isolation and made to believe that he is a tree, or a door, or a dream, he will act accordingly., it isn't faith that moves mountains it is belief.

Jahmel looked very pleased with himself, he was obviously enjoying at long last being able to tell of his years of efforts. I had to get Jahmel talking again before he noticed. I was just going to speak when he said:

"Perhaps, even with your limited intellect, Green, you may perceive something of the pain it will cause me when I put an end to my creation. When I kill Frank."

Kill Frank, the words bounced around my tired mind like a ping pong ball. The effect of this last statement seemed to shoot through Rhani like an electric shock. She spun around and stared at Jahmel. She almost sobbed. "Kill Frank! you can't kill Frank! you can't."

Jahmel leaned forward and took the gun from her hand and said, "Can't, can't, my dear, and why can't I?"

She was too shocked to speak, she just stood staring at him.

I said: "Why should you kill Frank?"

"Because, my dear fellow, who ever heard of people coming to worship at the shrine of a living God. If the God lives obviously they will want to hear him preach, follow him, become his desciples, it is only when he dies that they see the true meaning of his life. Jesus died for his beliefs and was worshiped for two thousand years

The real details of his birth and training would always be liable to be found out The Imperial will not attain its former splendour while Frank lives."

Rhani was still staring at him as if in a trance.

Jahmel said, "Poor Rhani, I have known for some time of your affiliation to the Mughal and your sympathy with the intentions of Minister Ghats. It is only through you that he could have learned of the possibilities of using Frank as a Messiah. Do you know the true definition of the word Messiah? It is Liberation of oppressed people or country. Frank would have served Ghats plan very well, wouldn't he? The Minister would have put the bridle of poverty around Frank and let him haul this country two hundred years clear of the dust. But I am afraid that does not fall in with my plans at all my dear, not at all."

I said, "There is one thing that is not clear, Jahmel, the switch, how did you switch the boys?"

"Ah, the switch,said Jahmel. "A very carefully planned part of the operation where I must admit I was helped by good luck. Fortune favours the brave, Mr Green.

My greatest fear was that Frank's brother would leave the area; if that had happened the whole thing would have been spoiled, all those years of work would have been in vain. It was that fear that made me bring my God to Earth sooner than I intended. I told Frank that his training was done and that when he next woke he would be amongst the people of the Earth. I mixed a drug with his food which sent him into a deep sleep. Earlier in the day I had dressed myself as a travelling mystic, a guru, and sent a message to his brother that I had news for him, and that he should tell no one but come to meet me that night. I had seen what clothes he wore and obtained matching clothes for Frank, then I brought him from the Forest of the Gods to the Plantation where his brother came to meet me that night. I had to perform the unpleasant task of killing him and making it look as if he had been attacked by a Tiger. It was essential that when he was found that he was not recognised."

I said, "Why didn't you just make the brother disappear and put Frank in his place?"

"Well," said Jahmel, "The Indian peasants are simple people, they are greatly influenced by mystery and magic. I wanted some way of shocking them and startling them, of causing them to talk and start the rumours that the Son of God had arrived. Frank, of course because of his lack of exercise was very weak. I made him do exercises, but it's not the same. I had to put him in the place of a healthy Plantation boy, they would have said, 'What is the matter with the boy today he looks pale and thin.' No, I had to give them some mystery to talk about. It was that night the good luck occurred. The Monsoon broke with a most violent storm, an old fashioned Biblical storm. The air had been heavy with electricity all day and the clouds were black and low, almost on top of the Plantation Hill. Frank's brother had come to meet me on what they now call the Burning Hill. I killed him, then rolled his body down the hill. I had laid Frank near a path that leads to the bungalow, . The rest of the story you know. The boy found his way to the bungalow and was accepted as Frank. When Mr Wilson returned with the body of the boy who was really Frank's brother they assumed that it was some itinerant labourer who had died so that God could bring his own Son to the Earth in the shape of Frank. This belief only really grew after I had arranged the miracles. There you have it, the only Mortal God this Earth is likely to see."

I said, "But Mr Wilson claims that he saw one of the boys on the Burning Hill just before it was struck with lightning."

"Then he must have been mistaken, you have seen the Hill, nothing could have survived. Now, Mr Green, my story has taken longer than I intended, you will have to accompany me on a short walk out of the Town. We will leave the Hotel through the back way."

Rhani said: "Jahmel you must think again about the boy; he must not be killed. Here is the opportunity that India has been waiting for."

"I am not interested in India, I am interested in me and the Imperial. By the way, my dear, how long did you know of my plans?"

"I never knew for sure, but I guessed. I knew when the girl left here all those years ago that she was pregnant and you must have been the father. I followed you to the Forest of the Gods once and found the tree house. I knew that the girl had gone to the Plantation looking for work with her son. When I heard that her son Frank had been chosen to accept the Spirit of the Son of God, and that a boy of similar age and looks had been taken as a sacrifice I guessed."

"And that was when you contacted the Mughal"

"Yes."

"Well that was unfortunate, but Frank will soon be dead, and there is nothing you can do about it."

"There is one thing," I said, "that you have overlooked, without me there will be no story, no Worldwide publicity."

Jahmel smiled. "I am sure that a little thing like that Mr Green will not stop Minister Ghats. Now it is time for us to take our walk.

Perhaps you would help Mr Green to his feet, Rhani, we don't want the problem of a corpse in the Imperial, do we?"

Rhani put her arm around me and lifted me to my feet. My head was swimming, it seemed like a dream as if it were happening to someone else. I walked slowly out of the room and into the hall, then down the stairs one at a time. The front door was open and I could see the traders in the Square. Safety was just a few steps away, but I would never make it and Jahmel knew it. I turned at the bottom of the stairs and started down the long corridor to the back of the Hotel with Jahmel behind me. Then I heard a clinking sound, a noise that I had heard before, but couldn't remember. Before I had got half way down the hall I heard a shuffling sound and I remembered what the clinking was, it was the sound of Ravi's medals as he ran. By the time I had slowly turned around it was all over. An ancient cavalry sword was sticking through Jahmel, its rusty top was pointing at me from his side. Ravi was standing behind him, great tears rolling down his cheeks. He said something to Jahmel, I only recognised the word Achmed . .Rhani's screams echoed around the hall

Jahmel leaned against the wall between us, unsure of which way to turn, then he fell slowly forward. As he hit the floor the point of the sword snapped off and spun up into the air and landed with a clatter beside him.

The old man put his arm around me and helped me out of the Hotel and down the steps, some of the others came to help him and they laid me on a cart. I was drifting into unconsciousness as Ravi started to push the cart through the Square, when I heard shouting. Everyone was running past us towards the Imperial. Ravi stopped and we looked back at the Hotel, smoke was bellowing out of the front door, as we watched flames ran up the curtains in the Hall, and the windows smashed. Smoke puffed out of the other windows as the fire got a hold of the dry old building. Everyone was shouting and pointing. I looked along the windows of the top floor, Rhani was standing at the window of the old nursery. She was smiling. When she saw me she threw back her head and laughed. I sank back on the cart and watched the smoke drifting up into the black clouds.

Achmed's wife was feeding me, she was cradling my head and pouring spoonful's of hot broth down my throat. Ravi was sitting in the corner of the room watching us. It was Achmed's house, there was no way of telling how long I had been there. During the next few days I drifted in and out of consciousness slowly regaining my strength.

Standing at first with Ravi helping me as he helped me in the Imperial. Then walking a few steps further each day until I was strong enough to walk to the end of the lane to the Plantation Road. The Road was packed with Pilgrims, with more each day. I watched them and wondered what had happened to Frank. If the Murghal had broken the story, if they had, Bill Steel would be going frantic trying to get in touch with me. He wouldn't think it very funny that the World News had got an exclusive on the greatest story ever, then missed the boat. The Plantation would be swarming with Newspaper men now, from every country in the World. I expect Bill would have sent someone else. It would be the end of my job, even if I had wanted to keep it.

Although I hadn't been able to speak to Ravi or Achmed's wife, I didn't even know her name, they knew when it was time for me to go. The pain in my shoulder grew less each day.

I was sitting outside the house one evening with Ravi. We were sitting beneath the canopy smoking his home-made cigarettes when he produced the keys to the old Mercedes and pushed them across the table towards me. Achmed's wife came out of the house and saw the keys and smiled and pointed to the old car. We all seemed to understand that I would be leaving the next morning.

I awoke early the next day and lay in my bed looking around the simple room in the old house with mixed feelings. I was excited at the thought of going home, back to my own country, to familiar surroundings and faces, but I was sad to be leaving Ravi and Achmed's wife who had done so much for me. She had saved my life and then nursed me back to health with hardly a word spoken between us. I dressed slowly and I could hear Ravi moving about in the next room. There was a knock on the door and Achmed's wife came in with my jacket and passport. There was a patch over the bullet hole and she had washed it, but the faded blood stains were still there. As usual we ate in silence, my whole stay at the house had been silent. But we had communicated with our hands and eyes and our minds. When the meal was finished I stood up, there seemed nothing to do but leave. I kissed Achmed's wife on the cheek then shook hands with Ravi, then he stood to attention and saluted me as he had done when we first met on the steps of the Imperial. Two empty petrol cans stood by the old car and when I switched on the ignition the tank registered full. I put the car into gear and pulled away from the house and bumped my way down the track. The old man and the woman stood in front of the house waving to me as I went and I watched them grow smaller in the rea view mirror.

I edged my way across the Plantation Road and into the back streets of Ranpure. I made my way through the Town to the Square for one last look of what was left of the Imperial. The front wall was still standing, black and burned. I got out of the car, one or two of the early traders shouted to me. I waved to them then walked up the cracked steps. The side wall had collapsed and the centre of the old building was just a pile of bricks and burned rubble. Part of the ballroom was still standing but that was all, the front wall and part of the ballroom. The monsoon had come while I was ill, perhaps the rain had put out the fire. Rhani was here somewhere and Jahmel, all their hopes and plans and dreams in the dust and the ash. The smell of burning still hung in the air. I turned to leave and trod on glass, it was the photograph of Jahmel as a small boy holding the hunter's gun, next to it was a Champagne cork. I picked them up and brushed the broken glass off the photograph, it was brown and curling at the edges but I could see quite clearly the small boy. I put the photograph and the charred cork in my pocket then walked down the steps and got into the car. I drove slowly out of the Square waving to the traders as I went, out through the back streets of the Town and along the bumpy tracks through great puddles to the Delhi Road. The smooth Delhi Road that led to the AirPort.

The rubies had been in my pocket for so long that they had become part of me. I had driven half way to Delhi before the thought crossed my mind that as I had not carried out my part of the bargain Jennah Ghats would want them back and my head with them. I had very little money left and would have to cable London for my ticket then hang around Delhi until the money had arrived from World

News, that's if they wanted me back. I may have had the sack already because I had messed up the story. It was several days' drive to Bombay or Calcutta, even if I had the money for petrol. I could drive past Delhi on to Punjab, that was much nearer, there was bound to be an Airport there, but where? I didn't have the money or petrol to keep looking. There was no alternative, I would have to take my chance with Delhi. I would go straight to the Airport and cable from one of the airline offices, then wait for the reply. It was dusk by the time I reached the outskirts of the city. I followed the arrow and aeroplane signs towards the centre of Delhi. The roads were very busy and the traffic was forced to travel slowly. It was sometime before I noticed the man running behind the car, there were no wing mirrors and he was running in a blind spot just off the rear side of the car, when I went faster he went faster, when I went slower he went slower, he was very good at it. I put my foot down and picked up speed then pushed hard on the brake and leaned forward, looking back down the side of the car. He ran for a few steps before realising what had happened. It was the big Negro bodyguard that had waited for Jennah Ghats at the Rain Feast. When he saw what had happened he jumped for the car door, but I was already in gear and pulling away, there was a bump as he hit the rear wing. I could see him lying in the road in my rear view mirror. It was obvious now why they had not come looking for me, or maybe they had. They knew I would come to Delhi and they knew I would come in Achmed's car. All they had to do was watch the Delhi Road for the old Mercedes and they had me and their rubies. I had the feeling that they would be more interested in me. They would be sure to watch the Airport.

The old car that had been such a friend was now an enemy, it would draw them to me and next time I wouldn't recognise them. I had to get rid of it I was feeling self-conscious already, like a gold fish in a bowl. I would have to get to the Airport on foot. I was stationary at the cross road near the centre of the Town when some British soldiers crossed the road in front of the car and I thought of it, who do you turn to when you are in trouble but your family and friends, and Sergeant Michael Jones was near as I could get to that in Delhi. I swung the car around and drove in the direction of the Union Jack Club. It took me a long time to find it, but there it was, the shabby entrance with the torn Union Jack dangling over it. I drove about a mile down the road and parked the car in a side street, then walked back to the Club.

The Club was empty except for a barman. As soon as he saw me he said: "I'm sorry, Sir, this is a Service Man's Club, no civilians allowed, regulations, Sir."

"I'm looking for Sergeant Jones," I said.

"Are you a relative?"

"No."

"It's all the same if you are, you're a week too late, he's dead."

"Dead?"

"Yes, Sir, dead. The wogs got him about a week ago, bit of a riot near the station."

I sank onto a bar stool and looked at him. I felt tired, weak and old. The barman said: "You all right, mate? you don't look too good, you'd better have a drop of something." He poured me a double scotch and said, "on the house, mate. What you might call barman's perks."

This final blow seemed to drain everything out of me, my mind was a blank, I didn't know what to do. I felt something tugging at the patch on my pocket and a broad Scots voice said: "It looks like the wogs have had a go at you too.", You look like shit.

It was Jock McGreggor, he said, "let's have another drink."

The barman said, "You know I'm not allowed to serve civilians."

Jock said, "Then what's he got in his bleedin' hand, scotch mist? Give us a drink and keep your bloody mouth shut."

The barman poured the drinks and Jock pulled up a stool next to me and said: "What happened to you then? You didn't get that lot doing a waltz at the Rain Feast."

I told Jock the story, the bits of it that would interest him, about Jennah Ghats and Achmed getting shot, and the Imperial burning down.

When I had finished he said, "You know Michael is dead?"

I said, "Yes, the barman told me. I came here to ask for his help, I must get to the Airport but the roads will be watched they will be everywhere looking for me now."

We had a few more drinks and Jock got up and said: "I've just had an idea, wait for me." He leaned across to the barman saying, "He's my friend and he's waiting for me. Give him a drink if he wants it." About half an hour later Jock came back into the Club and ordered two large ones. He drank his down in one and said, "Come on, it's time to go to the Airport,coach is waiting." He left the Bar without paying for the drinks and we left the club.. A great canvas sided Army lorry was parked in front of the Club. Jock was already climbing up in the driving seat, he said: "Jump up into the back as quick as you like. I've only borrowed this bugger from the transport pool and I want to get it back as soon as possible. If they find it's missing I shall end up in the Tower of Bloody London."

I climbed up into the back and fell onto the floor as the lorry shot forward with a jerk. I clung onto the side of the lorry to stop myself from rolling about as it screeched around corners and smashed and bashed over, it seemed like, everything that got in its way.

The lorry skidded to a halt and through a hole in the canvas Jock shouted: "Look lively, we're there, B.O.A.C.? terminal, all right."

I climbed over the back, as I reached the ground the lorry shot away from me before I had time to thank Jock. It carried on up the road then swung around a roundabout and came back towards me. I waved and shouted, "Thank you," as the lorry roared past Jock was smiling. He stuck out his hand and gave me the thumbs up sign, then disappeared in a cloud of dust.

I pushed the swing doors and went into the terminal building and up to the desk with a sensitive-faced young man behind it. I said, "I'm afraid I've got stranded out here, is it possible for you to cable World News in London? They will O.K. the money for the ticket and will probably pay your London Office, if that's alright."

He looked at my torn jacket and said in a smug supercilious way. "It's Mr Green isn't it? We have been expecting you, your Paper arranged your ticket some days ago actually. We were asked to fit you in on the first available flight home. Now if you will be good enough to tell me your Christian name and the name of your Boss."

"My name is Arthur and my Boss's name is Bill Steel."

He said, "Jolly good, Sir, if you would sign this, there is a flight leaving in," he looked at his watch, in 2 hours,. If you will go through to passport control I will see if we can get you on it."

Years of being a travelling reporter had taught me to always keep my passport on me and now it had finally paid off. I took it from my pocket inside my jacket and showed it at passport control then walked through into the safety of the Departure Lounge.

"Mr Green, Mr Green?" A fresh faced young girl in a uniform was shaking me. "Mr Green, your flight is about to leave, if you would follow me." I pulled myself out of the deep soft armchair and followed her through the swing doors at the end of the Departure Lounge. The rest of the passengers were strung out across the tarmac walking towards the plane. Night had brought a cool breeze and I felt better. My shoulder still hurt and I was dirty, sweaty and tired but the breeze seemed to wash me, blowing away the dirt from my body and the worry from my mind. I was going home to a cool land, to places I knew and people who knew me, and I was glad.

I put my hand in my pocket and felt the rubies, cold and blood red, an Indian legacy. A hostess ticked off my name on the passenger list at the top of the steps and I went into the plane, the other passengers were already seated, about two dozen in all and the plane looked empty. They stared at me as I stood there, at my torn and bloodstained jacket. The hostess had followed me, she said: "This way, Mr Green, there is a seat reserved for you."

We went through a curtain towards the front of the plane into the first class section. The girl said, "Sit where you like, Mr Green, you've got the first class to yourself." There were six seats three each side. I sat near the window and fastened my seat belt. A moment later the big door on the side of the plane banged shut and the engines burst into life. The great plane moved forward slowly and taxied to the end of the runway and stopped. The engine got louder and louder and we were off, catapulted down the runway. The lights of the Terminal buildings flashed by, the nose of the plane lifted and we left the ground. The under carriage closed with a clunk and we headed into the black night sky. I got a packet of Senior Service from the hostess and lit one, undid my seat belt and tried to think about things that had happened. It was the first chance I had since I had got into that old rattling Dakota at Stanstead Airport. I had come to India for a few days and stayed nearly a month. I had lived a lifetime in that month. Life and death, pain and pleasure, hope and despair. It was over now, but was it? would it ever be over? Frank was still alive and believed himself to be the Son of God. But where had it begun? With Jamel's affair with the peasant girl or earlier when he had bought the Imperial? Through all the daily visits to the Forest of the God's, his faith that he could make his own son into a God?

Jahmel was dead, but his ideas and plans for India lived on in Frank. If it hadn't been for his own sister, Rhani, it could have worked, he would have killed Frank after my final despatch to World News and his years of work and planning would have come true. Ranpore would have become another Mecca, it would still if I kept quiet about what I knew, the truth. What difference did it make who made a God or where he came from, or what motivated his conception? what mattered was his motives, his own belief in himself.

A World war had just ended in which millions died, if Frank could stop that happening again it didn't matter if he was found under a gooseberry bush. I lit another cigarette and pulled the smoke deep into my lungs and closed my eyes

... Rhani ...

"Hello, Mr Green we have both been looking forward to your visit for so long.' "She knew, had known, had guessed Jahmel's plans. Rhani, cool and beautiful, she had set out to convince me through her own beliefs, infecting me with a word, a phrase, with her body warm and firm, of belief that I caught. She was, had been the most beautiful girl I had ever seen, an Indian Princess raised to think and act like an English Miss. What torment she must have gone through studying English history, reading English books and speaking with an English accent when all the time her heart and nature cried out for India, for Indian people and the Indian way of life. That day at the Imperial, the last day when her brother had died, the brother she had given up India for. Had she tipped the oil lamps and lit the fuel as it ran down the walls to end her unhappiness, to finally resolve her life between India and England in death. When I had seen her at the nursery window she was smiling as the smoke caught in her throat. With death had she found peace ? .... Achmed ... Dear Achmed, a friend I would always miss. That night in the back streets of Delhi he had seen the worst that men can do to men, he had seen his own countrymen beaten and clubbed and still come out of the darkness to guide me, the enemy to safety.. I would always miss his companionship and loyalty. I would keep with me always the moments we stood together by the road on the journey from the Air strip to Ranpore and laughed together at the great hawk. How he had fought with me at the cafe near Delhi, how he had jumped up so eager to help me when I told him that Jahmel had tricked us, and had died beside his beloved old Mercedes ...

Ravi ... The old Soldier with pride and dignity, he had saluted and brought back memories of his youth. He had seen his son die, and with a rusty cutlass, a relic from some distant dusty battlefield, had taken his revenge with tears in his eyes....

Achmed's wife, who had pushed aside her grief and nursed me back to health. She had forgotten her own pain and had eased mine....

Majid, he had lived half his life with one arm for a few Rupees....

Charley, he had lived in the Tottenham Court Road and knew India - England, but knew nothing of the passions that had gone on all around him...

The little Beggar Boy that had no future, but whose past would revolve around a night when he knew what it was to dance and laugh...

Doctor Peabody and his Doctors and nurses, they risked their lives on the Lucknow Plains so that they could make the dying comfortable...

The Wilsons, who saw in Frank, what? the truth or what they wanted to believe....

Jahmel, he had made a dream come true. He had taken a child and instilled in him the belief that he was The Son of God. He had taught the boy with more diligence than any tutor at Cambridge and had produced a man-made Messiah...

Frank. He believed in himself, in his own ability to alter the World.

Maybe Charley was right, Europeans had forgotten the power of belief . Sophistication had weaned us away from it, yet dying men are saved by the belief that they will get better. And faith keeps alive men at sea in small boats or rafts, without food and water, for days or weeks when they should be dead. They believe they will live on, be saved, and if they have enough faith they are. Men on battlefields live when they should be dead from their wounds, because of their Spirit and Faith that they will live. Maybe Jahmel had uncovered something in

Frank that lays dormant in all of us, some unused corner of the mind that the rest of us will have to wait until evolution uncovers. Jahmel had died for his dream.

Jennah Ghats had discovered Jahmel's secret through Rhani and had decided to sponsor Frank in the name of India.

Sergeant Michael Jones who had wanted his name in the papers and Jock McGreggor who had helped me like a military Errol Flynn...

Frank, what of Frank, what was to become of him when I told the truth as I must. What happened on the Lucknow Plains, had I seen a miracle? Why not. Frank believed himself to be the Son of God as much as Jesus had, would he go on travelling the depths of India performing miracles ?

"Mr Green, Mr Green," the Air Hostess was shaking me. "We will be landing at Heathrow in fifteen minutes." A tray of food lay on the seat next to me. "You looked so tired we decided not to wake you." It was daytime and the sun was shining and the green countryside of England was beneath us.

I told the cab driver, Fleet Street, World News and settled into the back. I stopped the cab at Ludgate Circus and bought a copy of the World News with my last coppers. Banner headlines said: "GOD ON EARTH" and below that in smaller type, "The Latest Despatch from Arthur Green".

I got back into the cab and we carried on up Fleet Street to the office. I borrowed some money from the Receptionist and paid off the driver, then took the lift to the seventh floor.

Bill Steel was waiting by the lift entrance. He said, "What the bloody hell are you doing back here, how can you leave a story like that?"

I said, "Hold everything, it's a trick, a con, you've been had, we've all been had. He's not the Son of God, he's Jahmel's son. The son of man."

Bill said, "What do you mean a trick? What about those dispatches?" He ran to his desk and picked up a pile of papers.

I said, "Those dispatches were not sent by me, they were sent by an Indian Government Minister, called Jennah Ghats. It's a long story, a very long story. Is the old man in? I had better see him right away and get the story stopped."

Bill laughed and said, "Stop the story, you must be mad, circulation is going through the roof, and the advertising revenue has doubled. You can't stop this story, nobody can. The old man won't be back until late this afternoon. You had better go home and change and come back then."

"All right, but I need some money, I'm broke." Bill Steel gave me ten pounds from the petty cash box and I went downstairs to the street. I bought a box from the gift shop next to Mick's and walked up the road to the Post Office and bought a registered packet. I put all the Rubies, except one into the box and addressed the packet to Doctor Peabody, c/o the Red Cross, Delhi, India. I would sell the other Ruby and send the money to Achmed's widow. Then I took a cab home.

THE END

Lightning Source UK Ltd.
Milton Keynes UK
UKOW01f2028150217
294501UK00002B/142/P